FALLING IN EDEN

WILLOW ASTER

For Nate, who listens to all my crazy dreams and makes them feel meaningful.
I love you.

PROLOGUE

I hold up the silky black lingerie and sigh as I fold it and put it in my suitcase. At least Dane and I still have a sex life, albeit a sporadic one.

That's what this trip is about—time to reconnect. And in a way beyond the fast and furious sex during the cracks of our schedule. With his hours as a defense attorney and mine as an ER nurse, time is limited.

I zip up my suitcase and make sure I haven't forgotten anything of Dane's either. He'd said he'd pack during my night shift, but as I was getting home this morning, he was running out the door to meet a last-minute client and asked me to get his things together.

Cue the silent boil inside my chest.

I don't want to be this person. Constantly irritated. Bitter. And while I'm not a nag vocally, inside my brain is a running, *shouting* commentary aimed at Dane.

I hope this trip will be what we need.

I do a quick sweep through the brownstone, checking for anything I might be forgetting and washing the dishes Dane used last night. The kitchen clock ticks away, and my fury grows. He's late. He knows I get anxious if we don't get to the airport in plenty of time. I begged him not to be late as he was leaving this morning.

Stop. It's not the end of the world if we have to rush. You're lucky to even be going on a trip.

I lean on the kitchen counter and count backwards from thirty. I don't want to start out our vacation already mad at him. There's time. So we're not there in time to get a drink, not a big deal. We will probably just have time to get through the line and get right on the plane if he doesn't get here within the next forty-five minutes.

I put my head in my hands and think about how he was when we were first dating. I was working at the hospital when he came in one early morning. I hustled past him, and he tugged me back toward him, kissing me until I was breathless.

When I pulled away, my heart pounding from the kiss and also from hoping no one I worked with saw that, he handed me a bouquet of flowers.

They made me smile, and yet I felt wistful when I looked at them. Beautiful, but the edges were wilting and brown, and when I put my nose in them to inhale the fragrance, I didn't smell anything, but I did sneeze.

Dane and I laughed, and I thanked him for the beautiful flowers. "Dinner tonight?" he asked.

"Sure. I have a couple of hours after I wake up and before I have to be back at work."

He drew me closer, his hands squeezing my waist. "Come on, call in sick tonight. Stay with me. I'll make every second worth it."

I flushed again, looking around, and the nurses behind the counter stared at Dane with swoony faces. They still look at him that way when he comes in. "Maybe I could get someone to cover for me."

"That's my girl," he said, grinning. He kissed me again and backed away, smiling at me before turning when he reached the elevator.

"That man is sexy as sin," Dottie said. She was an older woman and usually too grumpy for conversation, but she always perked up when Dane was around. Sadly, she died that same year from lung cancer.

I remember not wanting to take off work. I

love my job and it helps to stay busy. I think I will always feel that way. But then, before I could talk myself out of it, I cleared my throat and asked the nurses behind the desk, "Would anyone want to cover for me tonight? I could cover for you this weekend."

"Uh, hell yeah," Dottie said. "I would love to have a weekend off. It's been ages. And from what I can tell, it's about time you get a life."

I cringed but nodded. "Thank you." And I turned and hurried off to see what I might have missed while Dane was here.

I didn't bother going to my tiny apartment to sleep before our date. My whole apartment was the size of the living room where we live now. I could never fully relax there, and I guess that hasn't changed, even in a bigger apartment. Both then and now, my mind is usually on what's going on at the hospital, and when I stay there, if I can't fully sleep, there's always plenty to do.

Dane had been wanting me to stay over at his place since we'd started dating a few months before, and I'd resisted it. I just wasn't sure what he saw in a girl like me. I still feel this way. Not because I'm not secure in who I am, but because we don't match.

He'd seemed crazy about me from day one, but I knew he must have limits on how long he'd be patient with a workaholic nurse still neck-deep in college debt. Before that night, we hadn't had sex yet, but he'd become more persistent. And I was tired of being lonely.

I didn't really fit in anywhere, never have, doubtful I ever would, and it wasn't like other guys were knocking my door down to get to know me.

Not really convincing arguments to start a relationship.

Or to stay in one.

I sigh and glance at the clock in frustration.

He comes through the door forty-one minutes later, his thick blond hair slicked back, his button-up shirt pressed, sleeves rolled up to his elbows. He's as cool as can be, grinning when he sees my face. I swear he thrives on my rage.

"Sorry, I cut it so close," he says, tugging me toward him and kissing my forehead. I pull away and he grins wider. "Shall we go?"

I have the suitcases and my purse near the front door, and I grab my purse and walk out the door, leaving him to take care of the luggage.

We're off to a great start.

———

I've settled into 17A, although I'm still wishing for the luxurious seats in first class. Dane is up there. He got upgraded as we were boarding and promised he'd change seats with me as soon as we were in flight. I peeked through the curtained-off area four hours ago and he had a mask over his eyes, mouth gaping open as he slept.

Another four hours have passed at least, and I'm cursing him for talking me into this twelve and a half hour-flight to Dubai. I wanted to go somewhere closer like New Orleans...I've always wanted to go there and it's not even a full three hours to fly from New York.

I shove my thoughts down and wrestle with the neck pillow. *We need this trip.* I repeat that to myself three times in quick succession as I turn toward the window. We need a vacation in the worst way. Both of us have been working insane hours, trying to keep up with the rat race that is New York. And we need this time *together.*

Sometimes I wonder why I'm still fighting so hard to stay in this relationship when I'm miserable most of the time. But he befriended me when I first arrived in New York, made me feel special. In the beginning, he wined and dined me, and I suppose knowing what he's capable of is what makes me stay.

And then there's the way he's been after me to have a baby, which is something I really want to discuss on this trip. I've been off birth control for a long time, and I haven't even been late once. Not a single pregnancy alarm or possibility, and I think that's for the best. I don't know how we could possibly consider a baby when we're at odds with each other half the time. *Most* of the time.

I want to stop trying for a baby and that conversation will be a difficult one. He can be extremely tenacious when he wants something.

I finally doze off as I'm telling Dane off in a dozen different ways about his cushy first-class seat, and I have the craziest dream. The ground and water switch places, and I'm swimming in the air and flying in the water. The water—or is it the air? —shakes and I hear the glub-glub of underwater screams that sound miles away. A pain pierces my head, and I open my eyes for a second to see that I'm on a plane of chaos.

An oxygen mask is dangling in front of my face, but the bump on my head must have been real because everything goes black before I'm able to do anything.

And then there's the weightless sensation of falling.

I scream for Dane, even though I know he's too far away to hear me. My stomach dips with the dive of the plane.

And then there's silence.

CHAPTER ONE

A dream finds its way into my subconscious so often that it's like reuniting with an old friend. The more time that passes, the more I anticipate it, and the more I miss the nights it doesn't come.

It used to be less frequent—maybe once a month—and then it held steady to once a week for years. But lately, it feels like my whole night has been filled with the dream. I don't know if it's true that dreams are only seconds or, at the most, thirty minutes, because this dream is so rich, so full, so *vibrant*, it can't possibly be in the blink of an eye.

I stand in a beautiful, lush place, the colors more vivid than anywhere I've ever been. The nearby waterfall is bluer than blue, the trees of the deepest green, and the flowers are out of this world. Every color of the rainbow and some colors that I haven't seen anywhere but in this dreamworld. Sometimes I'm more aware of my surroundings than anything, but often I see more of myself than where I am.

I'm holding a sword inlaid with jewels, a diamond on either side of a large oval sapphire in the tip of the handle. It's roughly five feet, made of Damascus steel, and I'm holding it like it weighs nothing. It's sharp enough to slice silk in half or to cut a coconut without effort. I don't even want to think about what it would do to a person. I'm skilled with the sword—it's a knowing that I don't have to second-guess. My arms are defined, and my abs are so chiseled I could bounce coins off of them —I know this because I'm barely wearing anything. A jewel-encrusted bra with a gold thin chain loops from the center of my bra, crisscrosses over my exposed stomach, and ends around the waist of my flowy sheer pants that cinch around my ankles.

If this were real, I'd be horrified by how little clothing I have on, but the me in the dream stands bold and unashamed. She does not cower or bend.

In real life, my body is soft and has plenty of cushioning. Sometimes I like being in the dream, hoping when I wake up, I'll be motivated to work out and get a ripped body, but it doesn't work that way.

Some nights feel like I'm just spending time there, grounded in my strength and the protective feelings that are deep within my chest. Other times, I'm spent from the energy it takes to be in this dream state. But what is most unusual and what torments me most about any of this, is that I know I'm not alone. It's like he's right there, just around the next tree, behind that looming flower bush, or just under the surface of the pool of water. Sometimes I laugh at him. Sometimes I'm mad at him. Sometimes I tease him with my sword, and I see the glint of light flashing across his.

But I never, ever see his face.

———

I smell the air before I open my eyes. Rose, gardenia, freesia, hyacinth, lavender, lilac...it's sensory overload but delicious. I inhale and blink rapidly as my eyes open to...all of those flowers and then some. I sit up on a floor of thick green moss and take in the color surrounding me on every side. My hand goes to my pounding head, but I don't feel any blood. I look down and besides the pain in my head, I don't have a single scratch on me. My traveling outfit looks nothing like it did when we left...my pants are far more colorful, and my flowy blouse shows more skin than what I'd normally wear.

We

I was traveling with someone. A man, I believe. I can almost call his face to mind. Tall, with blond hair and eyes dark as a midnight sky, but he's blurred.

I look around and stand up, walking toward an opening in the flowers. A white door with an ornate iron handle stands beyond a trellis of fuchsia, and I knock. When no one answers, I open the door. A bedroom with high ceilings, wooden archways over the windows, and more flowers are everywhere I look. The bed with white linens looks inviting, and I'm tempted to crawl under the covers, but since I'm trespassing, I call out instead.

"Hello? Is anyone here?"

I walk toward the next white door with the same iron handle and tentatively reach to open it, but the door flings wide before I can do it myself.

"Oh, you must rest." A beautiful woman with long red hair smiles as she gently places her hand on my back and leads me to the bed.

"But...you mean I'm staying here?" I ask, turning toward her.

"Yes. Do you remember what brought you here?" she asks.

I shake my head and she tilts her head, studying

me with her steel-grey eyes. She's stunning and I feel like I must be a mess since I just woke up on the ground in a garden.

"Where am I?" I ask.

She folds the covers back and I crawl into the bed, practically asleep already. This room and bed and the woman—there's something comforting about them. Something familiar.

"How long have I been here?"

She still doesn't answer, and I lie back on the cool pillow, falling back into a deep sleep.

CHAPTER TWO

When I wake again, I'm relieved to be in the same room as I was when I fell asleep. My hand goes to my head, and I give it a slight shake. Did I imagine that woman with the red hair? I get up slowly and clutch my head. It hurts to move, but I need to figure out where I am.

I go into the bathroom, admiring the clawfoot tub that looks larger than any I've ever seen, and the gleaming white...everything. I glance around and, yep, all white. I lean closer into the mirror, studying myself. Something is different. I frown, trying to figure out what it is, and pull the gown over my head.

I draw in a surprised breath when I see the definition in my stomach. How long have I been here? I was not this thin before.

I take a quick shower, tempted by the tub but not wanting to take the time. I need to find someone who will give me answers. When I open the closet, there are lots of beautiful clothes that are not mine. I flip through them to see if mine are in here too and look around the room for something familiar.

Images hover under the surface, the feeling of falling and the panic in my chest, but what is most concerning is that I don't know what's real. For all I know, I could wake up again and this will have all been a dream.

But my head doesn't feel right. The sharp pain brings me back to the present and I cry out, leaning on the clothes. Once I've caught my breath, I don't worry about whose clothes these are and just put something on. I can apologize later if I need to.

I open the door cautiously and call out, "Hello?"

Silence.

I walk down the long hallway, the white speckled marble cool beneath my bare feet. When I reach the living room, I smile at the furnishings. Whoever lives here really likes white. It makes the view outside even more vivid. I can see why they went with neutrals when the floor-to-ceiling windows showcase a garden so alive.

There are touches of stone too. Huge pillars stand next to a roaring fireplace and antique busts are displayed on shorter pillars lining the wall. It's a beautiful mix of ancient and modern.

I turn, glancing around the room, the feeling that I'm being watched making the hair on the back of my neck stand up.

"Hello?" I say again.

And then when I turn toward the kitchen, he's leaning against the wall like he's always been there. I gasp, clutching my heart as it speeds up. He's tall and muscular, with thick, wavy black hair and the deepest turquoise eyes I've ever seen.

And he doesn't look happy to see me.

"I-I didn't see you there. Are you—the owner of this house?" I ask.

His jaw clenches and a pained expression flits across his face so quickly I think I've imagined it. He nods and then says a quiet, "Yes, I am."

His voice is deep and melodic, and I want to lean into it. Even when his eyes seem to cut through me, I find myself moving toward him. He stands up straight when I reach him, almost a foot taller than me even though I am not short.

"I'm afraid I don't remember what brought me here," I tell him. "My head..."

His gaze roams over me from head to toe, and a flush heats my skin from the inside out. Before I have time to process what he's doing, his hands are on my head, touching the exact place it hurts. His hands are large and cool, and I close my eyes, the pain in my head dissipating the longer we stand here.

When he pulls his hands away, I expect the pain to return, but it doesn't. My mouth drops and I put my fingers where his hands were. "What did you do?"

"Healing hands," he says.

"That—*I* was called that." I frown. I don't know why that came out. I shake my head. "I'm not sure why I said that. I can't remember—how did I get here?"

"You were in a plane crash," he says. "You don't remember?"

"No. I-I think I knew I was traveling, but everything feels like a dream. Even this moment with you right now. Have I seen you before today?"

His eyes narrow as another expression flits across his face, and I get the impression he's usually far more vocal than he's being right now.

"I thought you saw me the first day you arrived, but I wasn't sure. And several times since. Your injuries were extensive."

"But I've felt fine the few times I remember being awake, other than that headache, which is...

gone. Unbelievable." And then what he's said registers. "How long have I been here?"

"A few months," he says.

I stagger back, the shock of that so strange I'm not sure how to wrap my head around it. "The woman with red hair? She's been taking care of me? Is this some sort of rehabilitation place?"

"I'm afraid there's no one here but the two of us."

I stare at him, unable to snap out of this stupor. "That can't be right. I saw her. I spoke with her." I put my hand on my head again and take a deep breath. I'd wondered once before if I'd imagined her. "I've been having really strange dreams. That must be it. But...I can't keep staying here. You've been so kind to let me stay, but I'll be going now that I'm...awake."

"As you can see, there's plenty of room. You should take your time and get your strength back."

"Can you tell me more about the plane crash? I'm almost positive I was flying with someone."

"I'm so sorry, Phina. There were no survivors."

My mouth opens and closes. I almost ask, "Am I dead?" but I realize how foolish that sounds. My eyes blur in sorrow for those screams I hear, for what must have been the people surrounding me as we crashed into—

A wave of dizziness sweeps over me. He reaches out and steadies me, his hands an instant comfort.

The expressions on his face do not match the comfort his hands provide. Even now, his eyes are foreboding, his full lips set in a grim line.

"Are you okay?" he asks.

"I really think it's best I leave," I tell him, backing away.

"You're in no shape to leave, Phina."

I get that strange sensation again when he calls me that. I think everyone usually calls me Sera, but my head is still foggy. Phina sounds right coming from him. The sensation is something stronger than déjà vu. It must be because he's been the one taking care of me all this time. How can I not remember seeing him? I don't even know what really happened to me. For all I know, he's not being honest.

Or is something far more sinister going on here?

"Did you kidnap me?"

CHAPTER THREE

"I assure you, I did not kidnap you," he snaps, running his hands through his hair.

I feel a slight twinge of guilt for assuming the worst, but I'm at such a disadvantage here, not remembering.

He makes an exasperated sound and my guilt changes to annoyance. But he says, "When you feel better, I can take you to the site of the crash. I'll show you where I found you."

"Why am I not in a hospital?" I grumble.

"There's no hospital anywhere near here."

"And no women with long red hair," I add.

"Not unless you mean the fairies," he says, his lips twitching slightly in one corner, the only sign that he's being sarcastic.

I roll my eyes. "So, you've been the one taking care of me all this time?" I flush thinking of what that might mean. I don't remember bathing besides the shower I took a little while ago, and I certainly didn't look like I had gone without. I put my hand on my throat and stumble back. "I will get out of your way." I turn and walk back toward my room, but not before I see the frustration on his face.

I shouldn't be angry with the person who's apparently taken care of me, but there's just something about him that stirs up all kinds of emotions. Emotions that feel too heavy, too deep for someone I don't know. Maybe I've been more aware all this time than I've realized. I should go back and try to get more answers out of him.

But I glance outside and the view outside my windows is so glorious, I can't resist going out there. My head is finally feeling better. I should go investigate a little on my own, see what's around here, maybe find the nearest town and make a few phone calls.

Who would you call?

There was someone. I think. But it's as if his face is in murky water and I can't quite make him out. That stumps me more than I want to think about, so I shake it off and slip on the elegant shoes in my closet. They slide on, fitting perfectly, and I walk outside, lifting my face up to the sky and breathing in the floral scent and the warmth on my skin.

Heaven.

I walk through the lush greenery and the flower blooms that are enchanted. I half expect a fairy to pop out of the garden, chuckling when I think of what—oh my goodness, how could I not know his name?—what's-his-name said about fairies. He knew my name, so we must have had introductions at some point. Add that to my list of questions for him.

The temperature is perfect, warm with a slight breeze. The gardens open up to a clearing, the waterfall in the distance creating the most perfect backdrop of beauty and soothing sounds, and I'm tempted to lie back on the cushiony moss forest floor and enjoy the sun for a while.

But something pulls me to keep going, and when I go past the waterfall, the air turns a bit cooler, flower vines draping through trees and ferns. There are tall columns with flowers wrapped around them, elaborate archways made from stone, and statues that look like they've been here for centuries. I feel like I've stepped back in time as I keep walking. And then I reach an iron gate. It's so tall, I lean back, and it just keeps going and going up into the sky. Beyond the gate is an extension of what seems to be an even more elaborate garden, which doesn't seem possible, but from what I can see through the bars, it's even more captivating.

I can't get the gate open and instead of letting it frustrate me, I walk alongside it, looking for any signs of life outside this barrier.

There must be neighbors nearby. And if the man mentioned taking me to the crash site, it must be close.

But the gate goes on and on for what must be miles, and I still can't see the end of it. I walk until exhaustion begins to set in, and I start to wish I'd stayed closer to the house. My muscles ache and when I reach the waterfall, I decide to sit down for a few minutes to rest.

"Nial!" I call, running through the garden, looking for him in all our usual places. "You'd better not be hiding from me again. I'll stab you with my sword if you are!"

Arms reach out and pull me into the canopy of wisteria. I look up to see Nial smiling from ear to ear, his twinkling blue eyes full of mischief.

"You know our swords are not meant to stab each other," he says.

I bite the side of my cheek to keep from laughing.

"Well, stop being such a jerk then! I've been looking for you forever."

"All of five minutes?" he teases.

"Long enough," I bite back.

"We're not due at the gate for another hour. Why did you want to see me?" His voice is like a cool spring day, and I shiver when he lowers his face toward mine. He's been doing that lately, making his voice all lovely and sweet and husky, and when he gets closer than usual, my body doesn't know how to react to all these new feelings.

"I heard we needed to be there earlier today. There's been activity near the east gate," I say, taking a step back and laughing when a flower bloom smacks me in the face.

He lifts the flower and moves toward me again. "Are you sure that's the only reason?"

I frown. "Yeah, what else would it be?"

His shoulders drop. "Nothing," he says, his tone different than before.

"What, Nial? You sound so sad."

"I'd hoped you missed me. I miss you when we're not at the gate."

"But we're together most of the time...even when we're not working."

"I know."

"Well, now you just sound sullen. And you know how I get when you're pouty." I level him with a glare, and he tries not to laugh, but he can't help it.

His hands go back to my waist, and he leans his forehead against mine, causing all the air to evacuate my chest. Something must be wrong. I don't normally have trouble breathing.

"You make me crazy, Phina," he says, his voice gruff. "I think about you night and day, when we're together and when we're not." His fingers lift to my cheek, and he caresses it softly. He's definitely never done that before, and that lack of air thing is very real and very disturbing. I take a gasping breath and he lifts his head off of mine, his eyes piercing as he stares down at me.

And then he does something really crazy.

He leans in and kisses me.

Fourteen and my first kiss. His first kiss too. I thought I'd be at least fifteen before that ever happened, but I am not complaining at all.

It's brief, but the feeling of it stays with me long after our lips part.

CHAPTER FOUR

I wake up in the bed and sit straight up. I know I wasn't here when I fell asleep. I look down and I'm in the same clothes I had on when I went on my walk. The shoes I wore are next to the bed. I get up and touch my head briefly, relieved it's still feeling fine.

I go through the sprawling house again, stopping when I get to the area where I saw the man earlier between the living room and the kitchen. But I don't see him, so I keep going, walking into the kitchen. It's beautiful, light and airy like the rest of the house, with fresh blooms hanging heavily over the edges of a large pitcher.

He rushes into the kitchen and visibly relaxes when he sees me. He brushes back the thick wave that's fallen across his forehead and looks at me with a mixture of contempt and concern. I frown at him, and he returns the look.

"You shouldn't overdo it," he says.

"How long was I gone?"

"Hours. I found you passed out by the waterfall. I wish you'd tell me when you're leaving."

"I don't even remember seeing you before today. Is that something I do regularly?" I ask.

"Leave?" he snaps. "Seems to be your specialty." He smooths his hair back and then grips the counter, not looking at me. "You're still healing from a head injury. There's only so much I can do —" He pauses, and I follow the slow glide of his Adam's apple as he swallows. He lifts his hand and waves it toward me. "This body needs time to heal." I see the clench in his jaw and my body tenses.

"Why the hostility?" I ask.

His eyes shoot toward mine and the air whooshes out of me. He starts to say something and turns and leaves the room instead. I stare after him in shock and wonder what I'm doing to upset him so much.

I stand in the kitchen like a zombie for a few

minutes, unsure of what to say or do next, when he stalks back in.

He opens the oven and pulls out a pan of something that smells delicious. I take a step closer, trying to see what it is. Some kind of meat and potatoes with asparagus and another green I don't recognize.

"What is that?"

"Bird with greens and roots," he says.

I chuckle at his simplistic answer, especially when it looks like an elaborate gourmet meal, but he looks at me unamused.

Someone sure could stand to lighten up.

"Can I grab plates?" I ask, looking around and going to the cabinet in front of me, opening it and grabbing the plates without thinking about it.

I feel his eyes on me and turn to see him watching me close the cabinet.

"Oh, was that rude? I'm sorry, I should stay out of your cabinets," I finish awkwardly.

"Can you grab the silver too?" he asks. He's still holding the food and waits while I glance around, waiting for him to tell me where. When he doesn't, I open the drawer I'd put silverware in if I were organizing this kitchen, and sure enough, I guessed correctly. "Looks like you know your way around the kitchen."

"Have we been doing this regularly? Having

meals together?" I ask as we take the food to the table next to another wall of windows.

"No."

"Oh. Well, thank you."

He lowers his head in acknowledgment and lights the candle on the table before serving my plate and then his.

"That's certainly a long gate at the edge of your property."

He looks at me sharply. "You walked to the gate?"

"Yes. I tried to see where it went, but no luck getting it open. So, I walked alongside it for a while."

He takes a bite and chews slowly, his features especially breathtaking in the candlelight, despite his perpetual frown.

"No wonder you were tired," he says softly.

"You mentioned taking me to the site of the accident. I'd like to do that, if you wouldn't mind. See if it jogs my memory or...if...I don't know...if it would help things make sense."

He nods, staring down at his food, and I give up trying to talk. My host doesn't seem happy to have me here, and yet, he doesn't want me to wander far from here either.

Maybe he's just not good with people.

"Do you have any friends nearby?" I ask. I guess I'm not ready to give up trying after all.

He stares at me for a few long beats and then shakes his head.

"Where's the closest grocery store?"

"Grocery store?" he echoes. "I have everything I need here."

"*Everything*?"

He nods. "Yes."

"Wow. I don't think I've ever known anyone that self-sufficient."

"I've had a long time to prepare," he says.

"You must be quite the skilled gardener."

"The Master Gardener designed it well and now it mostly maintains itself. Occasionally, I move things around to see if they'll flourish in different areas of the garden, but it's not my skill that keeps it growing."

I think that's the most I've ever heard him talk and I want to keep him going.

"I meant to ask—where are we? It's the most beautiful place. The gardens are unlike anything I've ever seen."

"Eden," he says, in a tone that sounds like an *of course* is attached to the end.

"Eden," I whisper.

I feel the slightest breeze across my skin, my shoulder blades tingling slightly, and I glance around to see if a window is open.

He studies me, almost expectantly, and I see his

shoulders sag slightly out of the corner of my eye when I turn my focus back to my food.

"This meal is delicious," I pause when I remember that I still don't know his name. "Please, forgive me if I knew this already, but...what is your name?"

"Nial," he says softly.

There's that breeze again. "Nial," I whisper, and I could swear he leans a bit closer.

We stare at each other for a few long beats and then he sighs, looking down at his food until he's finished eating. I can't help but feel like I've let him down.

CHAPTER FIVE
NIAL

S he doesn't remember me.

I thought when she asked if she'd seen me before, maybe something sparked her memory.

When she said she'd been to the gate, I knew it must have drawn her. How else to explain her walking all those miles when she's still healing? I thought being there would for sure bring something back.

When I told her where we are...Eden.

Nothing.

But what hurts the most is that I told her my

name and not even a flash of recognition crossed her eyes. The nickname she'd been the one to give me when we were little, when she couldn't pronounce my name right.

I've waited several lifetimes for her to come back to me.

There's so much I'd change if I could. So much I'd do differently now. I've spent every day missing her since she left, and even though I know she made her choice, I've been arrogant to believe our love was powerful enough to bring her back.

And then when nothing else seemed to be working and I had begun to lose hope, she quite literally dropped from the sky. I had to take drastic measures. That, I do *not* regret.

I watch as she goes by the fireplace and sits on the plush rug in front, drawing her knees up and wrapping her arms around her legs. She's so much stronger than she was a few months ago. I could hardly believe when she stepped out of her room this morning and found me. I didn't even have time to switch into the form that's made her more comfortable as I've tended to her.

She saw me when I pulled her out of the plane and swam her to safety. I know she did. She thought she was dreaming, and her lips parted as she whispered, "I've always wished I'd see your face."

I replay those moments over and over in my

mind. It filled me with such hope then, those brief seconds of familiarity, only to be dashed the next time she woke up in the garden room, scrambling back in the bed and looking at me in fear. I didn't know what else to do but try different forms until one put her at ease. The red-haired woman.

She still has the same fiery sass, the boldness that made me burn with desire for her as a teenager and the fearlessness that blazed an inferno through me as an adult. I'd thought the heat she created in me was wicked—my previous experience with fire having only been associated with the darkness we were expected to keep *out* of the garden.

But no, her heat was something altogether different.

Life and death colliding.

Ice and fire tempting fate.

Love and hate and hate and love, swirling until it's hard to tell one from the other...the line indecipherable.

If I'd known loving her would be this torture, I'd still do it all over again.

"Do you think we could go to the site of the accident tomorrow?" she asks, looking at me over her shoulder as if she's known all along right where I am.

"It's a long way. Do you think you should take a few more days to rest after your trip out today?"

"Maybe we could drive there," she says.

It's hard to keep my teeth from being on edge when she brings things up that don't belong in Eden. Remembering her life in New York when that has no place here.

"I don't own a car and there are no roads."

She turns to face me now, her face a mixture of confusion and shock. "No cars? No *roads*?"

I shake my head.

"You carried me all that way on foot?" Her voice is incredulous. It would be even more incredulous if I told her how I really carried her back. "How did you ever find me? Did you see the crash?"

This is where it gets complicated, and although I have always told her the truth, there is a growing web of lies between us that will only make me more uncomfortable as time goes on.

"I did see the plane crash," I tell her.

And that much is true.

"I think maybe I was traveling with someone." She frowns, and the knife in my heart that she remembers him at all and not me twists and dives in deeper. "Was everyone already...dead by the time you found me?"

Again, with the hard questions. Because the person she knew me to be was a protector above all else, and I did whatever I could to save and defend.

But she was the only one I saw on that plane, the only one I dived into the water to carry out, the only one I've thought about as I've nursed her back to health all these months.

She's the only one I've ever seen.

The protector and caregiver in her would never accept this answer.

So, I speak a half-truth because it's the best I can do.

"I believe so."

She swallows hard, her eyes filled with compassion. "That must have been terrifying and so heartbreaking."

The only thing terrifying about it was thinking she might not survive, and what breaks my heart every day is that she doesn't open her eyes when she wakes up and know who I am.

So, in a way, I do agree with her statement. "It was."

She rubs her shoulder blades and frowns. She's done this often since waking up here. As her redhaired nurse, I massaged her back until it eased, and I'm sure she's missing that now, even if she doesn't realize it.

"Are you hurting?" I ask.

"It's a strange kind of pain," she says. "Haven't felt it before. I must have done something to my back during the crash."

"I can massage your back if you'd like."

"Oh no, that's okay."

"I seemed to help your head."

She shoots me a surprised look. "My head hasn't bothered me since."

"Good."

She flinches again. "I suppose it wouldn't hurt. It's just weird being out here alone in the middle of nowhere with a stranger, but I guess we've been here for a while, haven't we?"

"Try a few thousand years."

She laughs and I bite back a smile. She turns her back to me again, and I lower to my knees and sit behind her, lifting my hands to massage her shoulder blades.

She sinks into my touch, and it takes all the restraint I possess to not press my lips to her back, tug her long black hair into my fists, and claim the body I've loved for so long.

I focus on the two spots I know are bothering her and send whatever healing I can to help. This is the one thing I can't heal completely for her, and my fear is that it will only get worse, the longer she's here.

Eventually she'll have to choose to stay or go, and if she decides to stay, I'm not sure she'll ever fully go back to what she was.

But I will be happy no matter what version of her I get, just as long as she stays.

CHAPTER SIX

I freak out a bit when he tells me his name is
Nial after I'd dreamed of a younger version of
him with the same name. And do I freak out
that it's about a first kiss in a place that looks
exactly like this? *Yes.* But I chalk it up to the weirdness that is this place. I'm sure he's told me his
name before now if I've really been here for
months and it's only been the two of us.

What is more surprising to me than anything is
that I don't feel any urgency to leave. Now that I'm
feeling better, I want to get outside and explore the

gardens more and go back to that gate and see what's beyond it.

I want to see Nial in his garden, learn the names of the plants and fruits and vegetables. How does he survive with no car? No trips to the grocery store?

I get a quick shower and stand in front of the closet, taking a closer look at the clothes inside. They're in perfect condition but no tags, so it's hard to say if they're brand new or not. I look for name brands printed in the material, but there are none. The textures are expensive, so soft, and in beautiful rich colors. I see something and love the shade of magenta, so I pull it out to get a better look and gasp. There's a jewel-encrusted bra with a gold, thin chain that crisscrosses and attaches to loose, flowy pants that cinch around the ankles.

I've seen this in my dreams so many times, in multiple colors. I hang it back up and rifle through the clothes, finding it in turquoise, black, white, gold, silver, royal blue, red, emerald green...

"It doesn't mean anything," I whisper. "Next thing you know, you'll be looking around for a sword or something." I bend down and do just that, looking for any swords that might be tucked away in the closet, but I don't find so much as a pocketknife.

I stand back up and take a deep breath, going back to the magenta shades. The closet is organized by color, which is so smart, but not something I ever remember doing. I finally decide on something that covers more than the bra and pantaloons, but it's still revealing—a fitted crop top tank and flowy matching pants. The back of the top dips down even lower and has a ribbon that crisscrosses and ties at the bottom. Impossible to wear a bra.

I frown. How could I have forgotten bras? And panties? I didn't wear any yesterday and never even thought about it. I go through the room, looking in every drawer in the bedroom and bathroom and back to the closet. There is absolutely no under-wear to be found. Insanity. I can't even find what I must have been wearing when I arrived, and when I try to pull up the memory, I can't come up with a color or style of what that would've been.

And if Nial doesn't even go to the grocery store, I can't imagine he makes special trips to buy clothes either. If there even are clothing stores within a hundred-mile radius.

I take my towel off and look at myself in the full-length mirror by the closet. My breasts are high and firm, my stomach has tiny ripples of definition, and when I hold up my arms, they don't jiggle underneath at all. I could've sworn they did before. How are they toned when I've been sedentary? I put my hands on my breasts, the fullness more than a handful, and I frown. I take a step closer to the mirror and turn, looking over my shoulder and gasping when I see that my thick hair falls to my *waist*. My eyelashes are long and full. I don't remember my eyes being such an icy blue or my red lips so plump, and my skin is silky soft and perfectly smooth.

What is in this water?

I look like the me from my dream and find it odd that I'd remember that, and that it's different from what I normally look like, when I'm still no closer to answering the nagging question of *who was I flying with?* Or more importantly, *who am I?*

I remember my name is Seraphina. And that I've gone by both Sera and Phina. Why do I remember I was called *healing hands*, but remember little else about my life?

Suddenly, I'm leaning over a woman in a stark, bright room and feeling for her heartbeat. The urgency, the need to be quick, as she's losing oxygen. A cardiac monitor beeps twice and then lets out a long tone as she flatlines. Seconds pass with no change, and I place my hand over her heart and close my eyes, calling her to life. When her heart begins pumping under my hand, the monitor beep returning, a rush of icy heat flows throughout my body.

I shake my head. Was that a memory or is my imagination getting the best of me? I couldn't have brought that woman back to life, I know that much. That can't be right. I'm losing it here.

In this paradise with a brooding man and no underwear.

Since I can't do anything to change my situation right now, I put the outfit on, and it fits like it was made for me.

I go to the kitchen, looking for Nial, and when he looks up, he looks me over briefly, his eyes flying back up to mine as he practically spits out his greeting.

I can see we're already on edge this morning. Great.

"How did you sleep?" he asks.

"I slept well, thank you. How about you?"

"Fine."

I exhale, perhaps louder than I should and with a heavy side of exasperation, because his expression softens. Not much, but I'll take it.

"I'm feeling good today and hoped if you have the time...could we go see—"

"Yes," he says briskly. "You should bring a wrap, in case it's cooler out there tonight when we sleep."

"We won't be back coming back here to sleep?"

"It's too far," he says.

"Oh. Wow. I assumed it was much closer than that."

He just looks at me and then glances down at the food he was preparing. "Eat some of this and I will bring enough food for our trip."

"I feel like I should change—this outfit feels too nice to hike in."

"Too nice?" he repeats.

"Yeah. I don't want to ruin it, especially since it's not mine."

"But it is yours."

I tilt my head as I study him, unsure of what these circles we're speaking in mean.

"That's really sweet of you to say, but...where did you get all those lovely things? Someone must have loaned them to you. So many pretty clothes."

A hint of a smile plays across his lips and then it's gone. "They're yours. All of them. Made for you, and only ever worn by you."

"I-I don't know what to say. Thank you. That is extremely generous of you. It will take a long time to wear all of it!" I laugh, but of course, he doesn't. "So, one of the designs...it's in various colors. A bra with a gold chain and...genie pants?"

"I'm not sure I know what genie pants are."

"I suppose not. It's just—"

He takes a step closer, the frown deepening between his brows. "Just what?"

"It's not something I can imagine ever wearing, but...I have this recurring dream..."

He goes still and stares at me. I blink rapidly and don't see him blink once. When I laugh again, he blinks, and I take a deep breath for both of us.

"What about this dream?" he asks.

"I'm wearing the same thing in my dream."

His Adam's apple bobs and eventually he says, "Interesting."

"Yeah. I thought so. What made you choose that?"

He frowns again. "Oh, I did not choose."

"I'm confused. If they're not borrowed clothes, and you did not choose them for me, where did they come from?"

"You designed them."

Chapter Seven

My mouth falls open and before I can get the questions out, he leaves the room. I turn to follow him out, a bit delayed, and when I go through the door to the other room, he's gone.

"Nial?" I call.

No answer.

I go back into the kitchen and take a bite of the colorful food he's laid out on a platter. The most flavorful burst of sweetness floods my mouth and I close my eyes, savoring it.

Delicious.

I sample everything, feeling like my taste buds have never fully lived until now. I can't stop smiling as I eat, feeling energy coursing through me. Whatever this is must be rich with protein because I feel so good. Besides the ache in my shoulder blades, I feel like a new person.

I wash my hands and go back to my room to brush my teeth, grabbing a wrap for later. I pull out the magenta bra and flowy pants again, wondering if I'll ever be brave enough to wear it.

"You designed them."

What could he possibly mean by that?

I return the hanger and walk back out, waiting in front of the fireplace. The marble busts catch my eye and I take a closer look, studying each face and wondering who they represent, if anyone. Perhaps they're just beautiful sculptures.

Nial appears next to me, and I jump. "I didn't hear you coming."

He nods, looking at the sculptures.

"Are they of someone special?" I ask.

"Very special," he says. He points to the first one and then goes down the line. "Gabriel, Michael, Raphael, Azrael, Jophiel…" He pauses and vs the last two quickly. "Hadraniel,

hen he says the last two, studying the The one of Hadraniel… "That one Is it a relative?"

He just smiles, his eyes lit up more than I've seen. "How crazy that there's a Seraphina," he says softly.

I shake my head. "I can't wrap my head around all the craziness here." I move closer and study her. "She doesn't look anything like me though."

He arches an eyebrow. "You don't think?"

I shake my head. "The eyes are all wrong."

He taps his finger against his lips. "I know. I've said that from the beginning." He shakes his head slightly and then turns to me. "Are you ready to go?"

"Yes, I think so."

We walk out the front door and it's a completely different view than the garden outside my room. A vast expanse of sky and mountains surrounds us, and it's still plush and green with flowers everywhere, but there's more space. The mountains look close enough to touch, but as we walk toward them, they don't appear to get any closer, even after what feels like an hour. Right after that, we reach a gate that looks different than the one I found yesterday—it's brass and sturdy but not as pretty as the ornate iron one. Nial opens it, letting me walk through first. Time drags. I find myself wishing we were walking in the garden. The farther we get from the house, the more I feel the sun against my face. The heat. My throat dries out, and Nial seems to know the moment I get too uncomfortable, handing me a lightweight bottle filled with cool water. I guzzle it, and I'm invigorated enough to keep going.

"Thank you."

"You're welcome." He takes it and puts it back in his pack, and we keep moving.

I try to think of things to talk about, but I'm struggling to focus on anything beyond putting one foot in front of the other.

It feels like we walk for an eternity, but how would I know in this place that seems to have no markers of time? I stumble and he's there to steady me. I look at him, my face crumbling, and he puts his hand on my shoulder.

"Phina, what is it?" he asks, his voice hoarse.

"I don't know. I don't like..." I rub my arms, glancing around to see anything unusual, or if I can put into words what I'm feeling. "Something doesn't feel right out here," I finish.

Tears rush down my face and Nial looks bewildered, completely at a loss of what to do with me. I don't blame him—I'm also at a loss.

"We can go back," he says. "I can carry you on my back and you can rest. We'll be home when you wake up."

"No, I can't ask you to do that. I pushed this. And I don't even know why I'm crying. I want to see—we've come this far. I'm just not sure I can—" I shake my head. "I'm sorry, I'm not making sense.

How in the world did you carry me all this way? How far is it?"

"I thought we'd walk until we got tired and go the rest of the way tomorrow," he says. "I knew it was a lot, but...you seemed so determined. I wasn't fully thinking of how it would be for...you."

That makes my shoulders stiffen, the knots tensing up, but instead of forging on, I sit down in the grass. "Because I'm broken. Just say it."

"Uh, *no*. You're not broken. You're just... without the usual tools of Eden."

"I don't know what that means."

He sits down next to me and pulls his pack off of his back. When he reaches out and hands me a small cake of some sort, I take it, sniffling.

"What is this?"

"It's something I know you'll love." He smiles now, a real smile, and my heart bolsters up at that. It also skips a few extra beats and tumbles into a few somersaults.

He's breathtaking when he scowls, but when he smiles, he's earth-shattering.

I hold the cake up to my mouth and the smell of lemons has my mouth watering. "I *love* lemons," I whisper in excitement.

He just grins.

If he'd look at me like that all the time, I'd move heaven and earth to do anything he asked of me.

My heart flutters. Must be all this fresh air

getting to my lungs and making me all dramatic. I smile down at the cake and take a bite. My eyes squeeze shut, and I shake my head slowly. "Oh, that is *good*."

I open my eyes and take another bite, glancing up to see him still looking at me with amusement. I hold out the cake.

"Here, you should have some."

"No, you enjoy that."

"You don't want it?"

"I have more." He pats his pack, and I'm so happy I don't have to share this deliciousness, I'm pretty sure I beam at him. He looks askance at me, which just makes me more pleased.

"I've had this before!" I say suddenly. I stare at the cake and nod. "I've had it before, and I loved it."

"Figures, that's what you'd remember." He sounds grumpy when he says it, but he doesn't seem mad.

Once I've finished the cake, I lie down, curling my legs toward my chest. "I'm just going to rest a moment." I hold up a finger. "Just one moment."

I think he might grin, and I like this new, pleasant side of him. *Maybe he just needs to get out more often...although if I get him out again, we're not coming back here.*

And that's the last thought I have for a while.

CHAPTER EIGHT

We run through the almond blossoms, the trees and their blooms creating a canopy overhead, and the ground below us covered with the ones that have fallen. He grabs my hand and twirls me around, as I laugh and collapse against his chest. Since he kissed me that first time, which has been a long time ago now, we've never stopped, and it's only gotten more intense each chance we get to sneak away.

He kisses me, and when our kisses become more urgent, I pull back and lower myself onto the white and pink bed of flowers, the sweet floral scent wrapping itself around me. He looks down at me and smiles, his expression a caress before he ever touches me.

"Nial," I whisper.

He knows exactly what I want without me saying it. We've talked about it before now, how ready we are, how our time at the gate won't be affected by this decision. We take our responsibilities seriously and that will never change.

"Are you sure?" he says hoarsely, and I love how deep his voice has become.

I nod and he gets down on one knee and then lowers himself on top of me. He's never done this before and now I know why—we would never have waited all this time if he had. The icy heat that tingles through me where our bodies touch is thrilling, and yet, I crave more. He lets out a sharp hiss, and I know the softness of my body is just as intoxicating as the hardness of his is to me.

His kiss is softer this time, tentative, and I run my hands through his hair, tugging him closer. He grins against my lips, and I groan.

"Sweet Phina, so impatient," he teases.

"Why must you make me wait any longer?" I wrap my hands around his neck and pretend to be sulky, but I cannot be mad at him. Ever.

"I do not wish to make you wait, only to savor this. We will never have this exact moment again."

I love how sentimental he is, how completely he loves. I don't know another his age who isn't more interested in fighting and weapons and playing games nonstop. Nial is excellent at all those things, as am I, but I am his true love. And he is mine.

"I love you," I whisper.

"For a thousand lifetimes," he whispers back.

"And beyond."

He kisses me then, really kisses me, and slowly unhooks the pink jeweled bra I'm wearing. The gold chain hooks onto my pants, and he unhooks it too before pulling my pants down my legs and leans up on his knees to look at me. It's the first time he's seen me naked since we were little kids, and his eyes are reverent.

"You're so beautiful. You make my heart feel like it will explode." His hand rubs his chest as if to relieve an ache and then he reaches out to touch my breast. He's been staring at them more often, his cheeks flushing when I catch him, and I enjoy how powerful it makes me feel that he seems in awe of my body.

"I want to see you." I lean up and unbutton his shirt and push it off of his shoulders, touching his nipple and down to the ripples of abdominal muscles that have been tempting me for a while now. His body has changed so much in the past year.

"You've seen me," he says, laughing.

I point to his pants and his cheeks flush, which makes me laugh too.

"Are you really sure, Phina? Promise me it won't change anything between us?"

"I promise it will only make us better," I swear.

He stands to take his pants off, and I stare, mesmerized, at what felt so hard against me seconds ago. As kids, we used to run to the water and strip down to nothing before jumping in. The first time we saw each other, he wanted to know where my sword was, pointing between my legs. I frowned and told him I didn't need something like that getting in my way. He shrugged and said it wasn't so bad.

"Your sword looks much *different than when we were kids," I say, my fingers going to my lips.*

He laughs and stands there proudly as I stare at him.

"Magnificent," I whisper.

He stands taller, his shoulders straightening, and that magnificent thing between his legs looks heavy and is pointing somewhere between up to the sky and out toward me.

"I don't remember it going that direction before." I lean up and wrap my hands around it, and he sucks in a breath. I love his velvety weight in my hands.

"This is how it always is now when I'm around you," he says.

I look at his face because he sounds like he's in agony. "Are you suffering?"

He closes his eyes and exhales. "The best kind of suffering."

"Do you know what to do?" Because for all the times we've talked about mating, we've never discussed the specifics, and now I'm wondering how this is supposed to work.

He nods. "I've been asking a ton of questions." He thrusts into my hands once, twice, as I watch in fascination. And then he removes my hands gently and lowers me back on the flowers. He kisses down my neck, and when his mouth circles around my breast, I jolt, leaning up to watch his tongue flick across my rosy peak. I feel a rush between my legs, and my heart pounds harder.

I whisper his name, and my head falls back, my eyes closing at the pleasure he draws out of me. This is going to be my favorite thing to do, I'm already sure of it. I gasp when I feel something between my legs, and I lean up, gasping again when I see his face there. He looks up at me while his tongue presses a long swipe against my center.

"Nial!" I shudder.

He keeps licking, staring at me for several seconds before dipping into me with fervor. I slam my hand into the flowers as I begin rocking into his mouth. He reaches out and puts my hand on my breast and squeezes over my hand, showing me what to do. I *moan and then feel my insides shake and quiver, and for a second, I'm afraid. It's all so much. Almost too much. But then the most amazing feeling washes over me and I let it, and even after it eases, I feel better than I ever have in my life.*

If this is mating, I never want it to end.

He lifts up and kisses my thighs, his lips shiny. He wipes his mouth as he crawls over me, grinning.

"Amazing," he says.

"It was amazing for me.*" I can't help but feel I got the better end of the deal.*

"For me too. Do you...feel ready now?"

"There's more?" I shriek.

He lowers his head to my neck, and his breath makes me shiver when he laughs. "There's more if you want."

"Yes, please."

When he nudges inside of me, it's bliss for a second, but I quickly change my mind about wanting more. My eyes fly open, and he's staring at me.

"I wish it didn't hurt you," he says. "I heard it will be much better after this." He leans up on his elbows and puts his fingers between us, rubbing me in soft little circles.

"Oh," I gasp. "That feels...better."

He pushes the rest of the way in and doesn't stop his fingers. And when he slowly pulls out and goes back in, it's better. The next time he does it is even better. And whatever he's doing with his fingers...

"Don't stop," I cry.

He smiles, his eyes lighting up. And then I start moving with him, chasing that feeling, and his eyes get wide. I'm about to ask if I'm hurting him when he lets out a sound I've never heard him make. His eyes roll back in his head, and he jolts and shakes, and I fear I've killed him when he goes completely still.

"Nial!" I cry. I put my hands on the side of his face and pray fervently for forgiveness.

We were not supposed to mate. Oh God! This was a mistake.

The guardians of the gate have one job: to guard the gate and make sure no harm comes inside. Outside of that, we rest and eat and make sure our bodies and our weapons are ready for whatever may come. There's been no mention of no mating for us, but we've been treated differently our whole lives, even among our friends, set apart because of our position.

Something that feels this good must be wrong.

But then he opens his eyes, and his body relaxes into mine as he gives me the most glorious smile.

"You're not dead." I sniffle and he laughs.

"We cannot die!" He brushes my hair away from my face. "I promise you, I am very much alive.

Phina," he says longingly, his nose brushing against mine. "I cannot wait to do that again."

And so we do.

He's right. It's even better the second and third time, and so many times beyond that, I forget that I ever worried about what this might cost us.

CHAPTER NINE

NIAL

The farther we get from Eden, the worse she gets. I don't know what I was thinking, bringing her back here. Well, I do know why I agreed. I want to do whatever she asks of me. But I should've known better. I should've realized her body could be in that in-between place. I wasn't sure before what was happening, but being out here, seeing the changes it's having on her body, it's clear.

When I first brought her home, she looked like my Phina, but there were differences. Her eyes were tired and there were lines around them. Her hair was to her shoulders, coarser than I remember, and her face and body were more filled out than before. Her coloring was less vibrant, the strain of hard work and stress taking its toll.

She was just as perfect to me.

My eyes wanted to swallow her whole and did not shut for days, the shock that she was finally back too inconceivable. But it wasn't even a week before her skin began smoothing out, her hair became shinier and longer. Even in the span of a day, I'd see a change in her hair. Her body shifted and contoured as she drank the healing waters and ate the fruit and vegetables she'd loved as far back as I could remember. I'd carry her outside and she'd stretch and sleep more, as if she was making up for a lifetime of lost rest.

She didn't look as sick then, even after just surviving a plane crash, as she does now. I have to think of something to get her back to the house.

She moans in her sleep, and I stop pacing and stare at her, wondering what she's dreaming about.

Do you dream about us, my Phina?

When she moans again, her body moving into a seductive stretch, I nearly come undone. Oh, how I've missed her. Her body. Her mind. Her smile. Her touch.

When she says my name again and again, and then, "Don't stop," I smile.

Come home to me, my love. Please, come home.

I don't hesitate. I lift her in my arms and extend my wings, flying us to the cliff just before the water. I want to take her the rest of the way, but she stirs, and I set her down carefully, moving out of the way and tucking my wings to my back before forcing them to disappear altogether.

I've never been without my wings for such long periods of time. In the beginning, when I couldn't bear to leave her side, I went too long without flying, which made me tense and edgy, the last thing I want to be around her. As soon as she started improving, I began flying while she slept, and that has continued.

I still feel like a moody bastard around her, but flying has helped.

I long for the time when I'm not hiding who I am.

If that day ever comes.

My hope is that she'll see where the accident happened and put it to rest. But if she must remember anything about that life, I hope she'll remember how unhappy she was.

She must come to these realizations on her own. I cannot sway her or lead her into knowing, or it will never work. I will lose her all over again, knowing it's my fault.

All of this is my fault.

CHAPTER TEN

I sit up and look around, disoriented, and turn toward a fluttering sound, but I don't see anything. I stand up, realizing I'm in a different place than where I fell asleep, endless mounds of sand around me. The air is dry, and I stretch before reaching behind me to rub my shoulder blades. They're hurting even worse than before.

"Feel better?"

I turn and see Nial behind me. As always, watching me, assessing. I feel that icy heat and rub my arms, sure that my face is red just from looking at him. I don't know what is up with these dreams, starring the two of us...but also *different* versions of us. Or at least, the more amorous versions of us. His lip quirks up on one side, and I could swear he knows I've had dirty thoughts about him.

I give myself a slight shake. Nothing has made sense since I woke up a few days ago. And the fact that I've lost time here that I can't even remember...all of it is overwhelming me.

I glance around. "Where are we?"

He points past the sand at the cliff ahead. "Just beyond that cliff is where I found you."

I swallow, looking up at the craggy rock face. "How will we get over that?"

"There's a path." He points to a barely visible path. "Or if you need to rest longer, we can stop for the night and go the rest of the way in the morning."

"I think I'd like that. I don't feel so well."

He steps closer, the concern in his eyes making me wish I hadn't said anything.

"I'm okay." I rush to assure him. "You must be exhausted."

"I'm fine." He turns and looks at the sky. "This is a good spot to stay. The stars will provide almost as much light as the sun."

I look at the sky trying to imagine that, but my

body and my brain are too weak to have much imagination...when I'm awake anyway. My dreams are another story. I nod and sit down and before I know it, I'm asleep again.

I dream he's carrying me, and we're surrounded by white feathers that shimmer in the light. It's such a beautiful sight, and I sigh into his chest, feeling sheltered in the safest cocoon.

I wake up and he's sitting next to me. I hear crashing waves and I sit up, looking around. The cliff is behind us and we're on a much lower rock with a flat surface, facing the ocean.

"You carried me over that cliff?" I ask, my voice coming out like a croak. I swallow hard, wincing. So dry.

He turns and hands me the bottle of water, opening the lid for me. I guzzle gratefully.

"I found you out there," he says, pointing toward the water.

I try to stand, but my legs are shaky, and he helps me up, his hands staying on my waist. I lean into him, my breaths shallow.

"How is that possible?" I whisper. It's so far out there. My eyes fill with tears as I stare at the water, the sensation of drowning suddenly gripping me. I clasp my throat, gasping for air, and his hands tighten on my waist.

"Breathe, Phina. You're safe. Slowly. Inhale slowly and exhale. That's it."

He turns to face me, and I clutch his hands, panicking. I try to follow his breaths and slow down, but it's not until he puts his hand on my heart that I'm able to get a full breath. As soon as I do, he drops his hand and takes a step back.

"Thank you," I whisper. "I...felt like I was drowning."

"Do you remember?"

"Only that feeling, the terror."

Pain flashes across his face and I know then that he's far more compassionate than he lets on.

"So, where exactly was I?" There's water as far out as I can see.

He turns and looks, shaking his head. "I couldn't tell you exactly." He faces me again but doesn't look me in the eye.

"Well, I can't imagine how you managed to save me out there, but I'm so grateful. And grateful for all you've done for me since. I only wish I could remember everything."

His eyes meet mine then and the turmoil brewing there is a physical blow. I put my hand on my heart and my face crumbles as I get another sharp pain.

"Phina. What's happening?" He puts his hands on my shoulders, steadying me.

"It hurts," I whimper.

"I should've never brought you here," he says, picking me up and running toward the cliff.

My eyes close and I drift off, my body shutting down. As I fade into unconsciousness, I remember something. I was a nurse. That's what that other memory had been about—me in a hospital helping someone, although I have no idea what I'd been doing in that instance...

I see blurred faces, one after the other—different patients at various stages of suffering—and me in my scrubs, sometimes navy or grey or surgical green, pinpointing the problem and quickly working to heal and save. The anguish I felt when I couldn't save them. I loved my job, loved helping people. And I was finally taking a vacation...somewhere exotic that I'd never been, but I was mad at whoever I was traveling with...we were fighting, I think. But I get the sense that we were serious about each other, and I feel guilty that I can't remember more.

It feels like another lifetime ago, but I'm almost positive it's who I was...*am*...who I am.

I fade in and out, certain that I'm dying or already dead. I open my eyes, and Nial places a cold washcloth on my head. I squint, thinking I'm seeing things. There are enormous white wings behind him. I rub my eyes and try to sit up, and he whispers for me to rest and that he's so sorry. I don't know what he could be sorry about. He keeps saving me, even now.

The next time I wake up, my skin is cool, and I

can take a deep breath without my lungs hurting. I hear a soft sigh and turn to see Nial in bed next to me. He's asleep and looks so much more peaceful, his frown gone and his brows perfectly smooth. His long eyelashes rest on his cheeks, making him look innocent and vulnerable.

I feel a rush of tenderness toward him, but I'm mortified. I wasn't ready, physically or mentally, to see where the plane had crashed. If anything, it just made everything worse. I couldn't handle it enough to even get back here on my own without him carrying me.

I need to leave soon. Once I get my strength back, I need to leave this poor guy in peace.

He opens his eyes then and smiles. My heart jackknifes inside me, and I smile back.

"You're better?" he asks.

"Much. Thank you. I-I'm sorry I pushed that trip. Sorry you keep being put in the position of taking care of me again. I'm going to take it easy a few days and then get out of your hair."

"My hair?"

"Yes, leave, so you can have some peace around here. It's obvious that you are a loner, living out here in such isolation. I need to respect that and get out." I say the last part lightly, but his frown has gotten so deep while I've been talking, I want to reach out and smooth the crevice between his brows.

"My hair is fine and so is my peace," he finally says.

I laugh at that, and he seems surprised, but he doesn't crack a smile.

"You cannot leave."

CHAPTER ELEVEN

"I remembered," I tell him.

He sits up, turning to face me, his expression hopeful. "You did?"

I nod. "I was a nurse..."

His shoulders sag, and he leans his head against the headboard.

"I remember the hospital and being crazy tired..." I stop when he gets out of bed and watch as he puts his hands on his head. "Are you okay?"

He turns, his eyes wild. "That is such a small part of the life you have lived. You really remember nothing else? No one else?" His voice has gotten louder with each word and ends on a roar. He puts his head in his hands and rubs his eyes before looking at me again, his expression bleak. "I apologize. I shouldn't have raised my voice."

"Do you know something about my past that you're not telling me?" I ask. I lift the covers off of me. "Is someone looking for me? There is a man that I-I feel I should remember. Why have I not even tried to find that out before now?" I get out of bed and glance down, the short, flowy white gown I'm wearing not leaving much to the imagination. "You put this on me?" my voice cracks.

"No one is looking for you," he says.

"But how do you know?"

"The world believes there were no survivors on flight TK 361," he says quietly.

"So, you're, what—keeping me here as your prisoner?" My hand flings out, and in the next second, I'm wrapping my arms around myself. He moves toward me and then turns, grabbing a robe out of my closet and handing it to me.

"I would never do that," he says. "Look at me, Phina. Really look at me. You know..." He stops and swallows hard, his hands moving to his hips as he exhales. "You know you have always been free to go." He looks tired suddenly. And like he's carrying the weight of the world.

"I don't know how I'd possibly leave. You don't even have a car out here!" I yell. "I haven't seen another soul..." I cover my mouth with my hand. "I'm sorry," I whisper. "All of this is just so confusing. You're right—I don't believe you're capable of that. But...there must be someone out there who is looking for me."

"Do you feel there is?" he asks. He pounds his heart with his palm. "In here, do you feel that someone is out there looking for you right now?"

"No." My face twists up and a sob comes out. "No, I don't."

He comes to me then and wraps his arms around me. I inhale his scent, the heady notes of bergamot and vanilla, and something peppery. The combination is seductive, and I sink deeper into his arms, my face against his chest.

"I can show you how to leave if that is what you want," he says.

"It's not," I say, realizing it's the truth. I pull back and look up at him. "It's not what I want. Not yet anyway. I just don't want to be a burden to you. Why do you live out here all alone anyway?"

"It's a long story," he says. He reaches out and pushes my hair back. It's gotten so long, it hangs down my chest and back in thick, loose waves.

"It seems we have time," I whisper.

"So it does." Something close to a smile lifts his lips, but there's something still holding him back. I can't tell if he's just a man used to silence or if it's me who puts him on edge. "I'm glad you're feeling better. Is there...someone we should let know you're alive and well?"

I try to think of names and faces of people I cared about. Even the faces of the patients I dreamed about helping are not clear. I shake my head. "I can't even remember my last name or where I lived...no names come to mind. Not even the name of the place I worked. There was a man with blond hair—which is no help in telling me who he is."

He flinches and goes still, his eyes darkening before he moves away from me.

I tilt my head, something suddenly clicking into place. "You knew the flight number. You must have a way to look it up."

It's a long pause before he nods. "I can get it set up for you. It will just take a few minutes." He turns and I move to follow him, and he looks back at me. "Why don't you...get dressed and meet me out in the living room?" His tone is sharp and my stomach dips.

I flush and wrap my robe tighter. "Of course."

I take a quick shower, glancing longingly at the tub. I don't know why I haven't taken the time to use it. Or what the rush is. There's no place to hurry off to—except to Nial. My face heats again, and I put on a dark green asymmetrical dress. It's flowy and soft and seductive, the common thread between these unique clothes. The neck is low-cut, with a ruffle along the V and shoulders, and it's so short in the front, it shows most of my legs.

I glance down at my legs, running my hands up my skin and feeling how perfectly smooth they are. Besides how awful I felt while we were traveling to the site of the accident, my body and skin seem to love this climate.

When I walk out to the living room, Nial is standing next to a small table he must have brought in here just for the laptop because I haven't seen it before. I haven't seen much of the house though, when I think about it. Now that I'm feeling better, I'd like to explore.

First things first.

Nial stands solemnly next to the laptop, and I sit at the chair he's provided. And then I look at the laptop and stare at it.

"I don't think I know how to use this." I look up at him. "I think I used to be able to. Why would I know that but not know the first thing about what to do with it now?"

He starts to say something and then presses his lips together. "Let me see if I can get us started," he finally says. He presses a few buttons and I swear, it's like I know it's a laptop, but everything else, all the specifics, they're completely gone.

An article about the flight comes up, and he steps back, letting me read it in peace. The gist is that all two hundred and eighty-six passengers were killed in flight TK 361 from New York to Dubai. I let that settle for a moment—all those people. And then, New York? Dubai? I feel sadness that so many lives were lost, but beyond that, nothing. I don't feel a connection to any of it. I continue reading.

Rescue crews searched the Persian Gulf for weeks following the crash, and while many bodies were found, not all have been recovered. Although the Gulf is shallower than most large bodies of water, there are still deep areas, and that, combined with the change in color of the water, make it difficult. More than sixty species of sharks have been known to reside in the Gulf...

My hands start trembling and I scoot the chair back, needing to take a break.

"Does it have a list of the names of the people who were on the flight?" I ask, standing up and moving away.

"That particular article does not, but I was able to find something about a month ago." He pulls up a list of names and I sit back down, going through the long list of names. I go through it twice, not noticing my name the first time. But the second time through, I stop on Sera Kristof.

I point at it and Nial leans in and then nods. I go through the list a few more times, stopping on a few to see if I feel anything, but it's just blank. I don't recognize anyone.

"Nothing," I say. "I thought I was flying with

someone, but I must have been alone. No one sounds familiar. But then again, neither does Kristof."

"You're sure?" he asks.

"Yes." I look at it again, going slowly over every name, but nothing changes. "But maybe I can find out where I worked." I stare at the laptop again and then he comes over and types it in for me.

My name comes up, but it's not a hospital website like I'm expecting. It's an obituary and when I click on it, so little is said about me, I'm not sure it's really me.

And then I exhale sharply. "That's *not* me. Look at the date. That's a year ago."

He stands up abruptly and then comes back, typing in a few different searches. S. Kristof, Seraphina Kristof, Sera Kristof, R.N. The only thing that comes up is with Sera Kristof, R.N. When I read the brief clip, I draw in a sharp breath. It says that Sera worked at New York-Presbyterian a year ago and died in a plane crash.

"I don't understand."

Nial places his hands on the table and takes a deep breath before looking at me. "There's something I need to tell you."

CHAPTER TWELVE

H e sits down in the chair behind me, and I turn to face him.

"I haven't been truthful about how long you've been here. Not intentionally," he hurries to add when I start throwing questions at him.

"What is that supposed to mean?" I demand.

"Time is different here," he says. "I know that is hard to understand, and I wish I could explain it better, but it's the truth. I don't really know how long it's been. If that is you, and I believe it is, you must have been here a year."

"That makes no sense," I snap. I tap at the date on top of his laptop. "All you have to do is look right here and you'll see the date."

He shakes his head. "I haven't even had a laptop until you asked me to—" He clamps his mouth shut.

"What were you going to say? Until I what?"

"It won't make any more sense for you to hear what I was about to say. Until you remember, there's nothing I can do to explain it to you."

"What is there to explain exactly?" I laugh, and I know I sound crazy. "And what if I never remember?"

"Tell me what you dreamed about while we were going to the water," he says, leaning forward.

"What? Oh..." I put my hand to my throat and know my skin is getting pink again. "Why does that matter?"

"Maybe it will help to talk about it?"

"I hardly think a dream about two horny adolescents will help." I look up at the ceiling, embarrassed that I even said that much.

"You'd be surprised," he says quickly.

I glance at him again, my eyes narrowing. "How did you know I was dreaming?"

"You said some things." He shrugs. "You said my name a lot. You whispered, 'don't stop,' and 'you're not dead.'" His eyes gleam, light and easy again, and I would think he's enjoying this if his tone and firm mouth weren't so serious.

I have to put my hands on my cheeks to try to cool them off. "It was a silly dream."

"Would you tell me everything you remember?"

I think about how passionate they were in my dream, how real it felt, like I was reliving a moment that had been important to me. I frown. When I try to remember *my* first time having sex, I can't. All I remember is them.

"You said they were adolescents? So, you saw them?" He tries to lead me into talking, but I'm too embarrassed to tell him all that...even though it feels like he knows.

"It didn't make any sense. We were young and—"

His eyes light up when I say *we*.

"It obviously wasn't us." I laugh awkwardly. "But it looked like the younger versions of us, and we were...happy together."

His lip twitches and I roll my eyes, knowing he's trying not to laugh. "What were we doing?"

"We were having sex for the first time," I say through gritted teeth.

"Ahh. Yes. Good times." He grins, and I wish I could throw something at him. "Does anything else stand out?"

"I still don't understand how this could help anything, talking about a dream that—"

"Sometimes dreams tell us more than anything else can. When our minds are at rest, valuable information can come in."

"There was a sense of foreboding, despite how excited I—*they* were—she seemed afraid that what they were doing was wrong. Something about the gate."

His body goes on alert. "What about the gate?"

"I don't really understand that part. It was like we were guardians of some sort...and had been set apart our whole lives. She worried that maybe being...intimate would prevent them from doing the job they were supposed to do."

It's like a wall drops between us, a huge invisible divide that may as well be ten feet tall and ten feet deep. He stands up and walks out of the room, leaving me sitting there wondering what I've said wrong now.

Eventually, I go back to my room and step outside my glass doors, sitting in the garden. The air is so much clearer here. So different than how it felt to walk toward the accident. The longer I'm out here, the more invigorated I feel. The urgency from before fades away. Nothing is complicated out here. Or tense. Even the weirdness with Nial seems small, and I know we can work it out. I don't think about any pasts out here, in dreams or otherwise, just soak up the sunshine, the gentle breeze, and the rich fragrance of all the blooms.

I walk inside later—what Nial said about time must be true because I have not known the time since I got here, and I haven't cared to. I wonder if I've always been that way or if it's this place.

I decide it *is* time for me to venture through the house. So far, I've only seen my room, the long hallway, the living room, and the kitchen.

I go through the doorway from the living room and am surprised to find a whole separate wing that's much larger than my side of the house. The first room to the left is a library. I gasp when I walk inside, turning in circles when I see books from the floor to the vast ceiling on every side. There are tall, white iron ladders that slide around the room to reach the books that are too high. I walk over to the closest shelf and look at the books, picking one up that looks well loved.

I smile when I see the cover. It's familiar, a young girl engraved in brown leather on the cover, and I flip through the pages, remembering the story of how she finds an elephant and they become friends. I get lost in the story, but eventually put it back and take out another, glancing around the rest of the room. There's a desk in the center of the room, and besides a large pen with a cream feather on the end and a cream leather journal, it's clear. I'm tempted to crack open the journal, but since I'm already snooping in a part of the house that Nial has never said I could enter, I stick with one crime at a time.

I grab another book, piling it on the other one, and go back out, already excited for the next time I can visit this room. Across the hall is a sitting area with a grand piano, a harp, and a guitar. I'm drawn to the instruments, but again, I'd rather speak with Nial about coming on this side of the house than have him catch me playing his instruments. When I step into the hall again, I almost turn back to the living room, but I'm compelled to keep looking.

The next room has a large bed with dark linens and a light leather couch. It's more masculine than my room, and I wonder if it's Nial's. But it looks like it hasn't been touched. If he makes his bed that perfectly every day, I'm impressed. Across the hall is another bedroom very similar to the last, but instead of a couch, this one has a large desk and several bookshelves. I look for any personal effects and see a man's clothes in the closet. They're different than Nial's clothes. Almost like costumes but in excellent condition and very well made.

One after the other, I go through bedrooms that seem like they're kept in perfect condition should whoever lived here before ever come back. And then I reach a room that takes my breath away. A white four-poster bed with silver and gold touches throughout the room. The walls are white woodwork and marble inlaid with shimmering gold leaf. A huge crystal chandelier hangs from the high ceilings, and wooden arches are above every window. It's the most beautiful room I've ever seen.

I back out of it and see that there's one last room. I peek inside and there's no sign of Nial, but this is obviously where he stays. His room is smaller than the rest, the large bed with white linens to the left when I walk in. The bed is made, but it's not as perfect as the other beds were, and I see a pair of his shoes in the corner. I go rest of the way into the room, taking in the small desk in the corner, a lamp on top, and something that looks like a compass. But when I turn to face the bed, the blood drains from my face.

Hanging over the bed is a painting that's at least five feet tall.

A woman...or...an angel actually. Now that I take a closer look, I see the hint of wings tucked against her back. She's smiling, and her eyes are the iciest blue. She's wearing a sheer white flowy gown, the outline of her breasts showing through the material, and hints of thin gold chains are on her neck and under her dress, crisscrossing over her stomach. A sword is sheathed at her waist.

She looks just like me.

CHAPTER THIRTEEN

"What do you think of her?" Nial asks.

I jump out of my skin and turn to look at him. He's waiting for my answer, and I'm so glad he doesn't seem mad I'm in his personal space, his question doesn't register right away.

"She's lovely."

He nods and still seems to be waiting for me to say something else.

"She looks familiar," I say, looking back at her. Maybe I just imagined that she looks like me. No, she really, *really* does.

"Someone you know?" he asks.

"Have I—been here before?" I whisper.

He takes a step closer, his lips parting as he scans my eyes, his gaze dropping to my lips before reluctantly meeting my eyes again.

"Do you remember?" he whispers.

My whole body feels like it's on the precipice of something, leaning at the very edge and about to fall.

"Or maybe this is a new painting?" I ask.

"It is not a new painting," he says emphatically.

"What made the artist choose to give her wings and a sword?"

He sighs and I feel like I'm asking all the wrong questions. He seems agitated now.

"Your house is very beautiful." I choose another direction since I feel him clamming up the longer we stand here. "So big. Did you grow up in this house?"

"In a way. This was a meeting place among me and my..." He drifts off and he shakes his head. "You know what, I cannot talk about it. I keep trying to figure out ways, but the truth is, I cannot."

"Oh, I'm sorry. Because it's painful to talk about?"

"Among other reasons," he says.

"May I ask how old the painting is?"

He glances up at the ceiling, his patience with me obsolete. "Thousands of years old."

"Thousands?" I snort, laughing. When he doesn't laugh, my mouth drops open. "You're serious?"

"Completely."

"But it's in perfect condition."

"I try to take care of my things," he says.

"I noticed. The house is spotless. I don't know how you keep it so tidy by yourself."

"Thank you." He lowers his head.

"I'm sorry, can I just ask one more thing?"

His exhale is ragged. "If you must."

"Did she ever see this painting? The woman in the picture?"

He looks at the painting, and then he turns back to me and stares at me for what feels like an eternity.

"No," he says finally. "She did not."

And he turns and walks out on me for a second time, leaving me staring at the woman.

———

I don't see him again that night, and I look throughout the house for him. When my stomach is growling, I go to the kitchen and pull out some of the meats and cheeses and pour a glass of wine from an already opened bottle. After I'm full and have cleaned up the kitchen, I go back to the room that had the instruments and go to the harp. Since Nial doesn't seem to be here right now, what will it hurt if I play?

I go to the harp first and run my hand over the strings. And then I sit in the chair near it and situate the harp between my legs, resting it on my right shoulder. As far as I can remember, I've never played the instrument, but when I close my eyes, feeling the strings under my fingers, my hands begin to move, and the most beautiful music pours out of me.

I'm so lost in how good it feels to play, how the melodies seem to wash everything else away, the things that don't make sense, the things I can't remember, the weird way Nial seems to want me to say things I can't say...I let all of those feelings transport into music and enjoy the healing it brings.

When my fingers are tired, my eyes bleary from the long day, I set it down gently and stand up. Nial is in the doorway and his face is wet with tears. He wipes them hurriedly and turns away, hurrying toward his room and shutting the door behind him.

I don't know what to do. How to make anything better.

So, I go to bed and hope tomorrow will be a better day.

· · ·

I run to the gate, Nial on my heels, feeling the breeze on my face and not a care in the world. Ever since we were intimate, I've felt like I'm walking on air. I'm so happy, and his expression reflects the same joy. Michael and Raphael have teased him mercilessly, but he just laughs it off. He's never hidden how he feels about me, and now, he's even more open with his kisses and hugs when we're around everyone.

We get to the last stretch of fruit trees and the hanging floral vines before the gate, and I come to an abrupt halt when I see Gabriel and Jophiel in the distance.

"What's the matter?" Nial asks behind me.

"Gabriel and Jophiel are waiting for us. Do you think they know about us?"

"I'm sure they've heard, but I don't see why it would matter to them," he says.

Gabriel and Jophiel are older and more particular about how Hadraniel and I conduct ourselves. I always roll my eyes when they're not looking when I hear them call him that, which makes Nial squirm, trying not to laugh. I've called him Nial since we were little, when I couldn't spit out Hadraniel, and everyone else eventually called him Nial too, but Gabriel and Jophiel would never resort to nicknames.

I take a deep breath and walk the rest of the way,

bowing my head in reverence. Nial does the same next to me.

"Good morning," Jophiel says. "Did you enjoy your break?"

"We did," Nial says, his smile wide.

Enjoy is putting it mildly. Nial and I rose to the stars and the sun and the moon when we joined today. We discovered how incredibly sensitive our wings are—something I would've never guessed if Nial hadn't traced his finger over every vein and feather of my set. I sang louder than the songs I play on the harp, and for all I know, the entire garden heard my pleasure.

I'm certain my face is flushed when I meet Jophiel's eyes. She is exceptionally beautiful, her hair long and silky and bright yellow, her wideset green eyes, and her berry red lips. Her skin is the color of bronze, and she walks with such dignity and grace, I sometimes feel like a foolish child in her presence.

Her face is stern and I'm waiting for her to reprimand us for the way we've spent our breaks from the gate. We guard over it night and day and haven't had any outside conflict in years.

"There was activity earlier today," she says. "Too close for our liking. Did you sense anything on your last shift?"

I'm shaking my head even as I'm replaying the events of our night. I stop suddenly and glance at Nial. "There was a stronger breeze that picked up *early this morning. We discussed it, but it was gone in the next moment."*

Gabriel nods. "Dagon has been slithering around. Nothing too close...yet. But I don't like it. He stays on the periphery, probably just enough to make his annoying presence known..."

Nial and I glance at each other uneasily. We've heard about Dagon, but we've never encountered him personally. I don't like that he was this close, and I didn't sense more than a strong breeze that didn't seem all that out of the ordinary.

I've been too distracted. I love Nial with all my heart, but I can't put everyone at risk by losing sight of my responsibilities. Neither of us can.

Too much is at stake.

Chapter Fourteen
Nial

S ometimes the guilt is more than I can take. My love, my lust, my single-minded obsession with all things *Seraphina* is what banished us from the garden and drove her away from me for good.

Not only that, but it permanently changed mankind.

One moment of weakness.

I have had to live with that decision, day in and day out, for thousands of years. Sometimes I think I should have chosen the path Phina took. But I couldn't do it, and now that she's back, I'm glad I didn't.

I fly until my aggression and anguish are spent, circling over the house, and swooping down occasionally to catch the sight of her sleeping. I'm not sure how much longer I can keep the truth from her without exploding. It's so different now than when she first arrived, when it was as if the world and the crash had taken its toll on her body, and she needed so much sleep and the nutrients of the garden back in her system. She's improved so much. The conversations we've been having—that's something I never imagined happening again. And at times, I'm so overwhelmed with emotion, I don't think I can get the words out. Other times, the guilt is paralyzing. And then I get angry...angry at Dagon, angry at myself, even angry with her for the choice she made, and I know it's only serving to push her away, rather than do the one thing in this world I still desire most of all: to live out our lives together in love.

I check to make sure she's sleeping soundly again before I go check the border around the gate. The way she got so sick the moment we stepped beyond the border concerns me. I want to attribute that to how long she's been away, how long her body has been adjusted to that landscape versus this one, but I'm concerned that there's more to it than that.

I fly toward the most beautiful parts of Eden, the part that Phina and I can never cross now. I think the loss of that is what grieved Phina more than anything, certainly more than losing me. I've grieved that loss as well, but it's eased through the years. I'm grateful to have the portion I have, although I miss my friends more than I can say.

Everything looks fine over there, and I make my way across the sky to the farthest end, where Phina and I walked out of the gate and beyond. I hover just at the entrance, taking my time to assess any stirrings of unease.

Nothing feels unusual. So eventually, I head back to the house, already eager to see her again. When I look in her windows, I watch the way she tosses in her sleep, and I go into her room, unable to not comfort her when the dreams torment her.

I wrap my arms around her, and she stills right away. *Did he comfort you when you had bad dreams?* She hasn't mentioned much about him, other than thinking she was traveling with someone. I wonder if she's dreamed about him the way she dreams about me.

I close my eyes, trying to put a stop to these ridiculous thoughts.

She's here.

With me.

Now, if she will only remember me.

CHAPTER FIFTEEN

I wake up the next morning feeling more subdued. These dreams are beginning to distress me. The recurring dream before I ever came here is one of the few things that has stayed with me from my life before. But with this new revelation about time—who's to say I'm not remembering that wrong? Maybe that dream only began when I arrived here, and my memory is still disjointed from a head injury.

But why these dreams now that are so real? And why does it feel like something bad is about to happen to the lovers? Something I want to warn them about...but how could I ever imagine I could fix anything?

The painting in Nial's room. The sculpture of Seraphina.

My thoughts weigh me down and my body even feels sluggish.

I need to find Nial and demand answers.

He knows something. I know he does.

And this nonsense that he can't tell me...I just don't buy it.

I get ready for the day, taking a little more time on my appearance. I put on a beautiful royal blue dress and stare at myself in the mirror for a long time, seeing the young Phina in my dream and the warrior over Nial's bed looking back at me. I step closer to the mirror and study my face, my skin, my hair, my body. Is she taking over my body and soon she will take over my mind?

I step back, knowing what I need to do. Even before seeing Nial. I need to go to the gate, to the opening that I couldn't get through when I first walked alongside it. It's where Gabriel and Jophiel confronted Phina and Nial, and I want to see it in the daylight while the dream is fresh in my mind.

I slip out my door. There's no reason to keep Nial from knowing where I am, but I'm hesitant nonetheless, wanting to do this on my own.

I'm stronger than I was the last time I made this walk, and it doesn't seem as long as it did before to reach the waterfall and to go through the various fields and gardens. Just seeing the gate up ahead, my spirits lift. And when I reach it, I take a deep breath, feeling the crisper air, the vibrance that is even more heady just on the other side. I put my hands on the ancient metal, a slight buzz charging inside me, and the yearning to walk through is so powerful, I start to cry.

I close my eyes and feel the bond to this earth so strong, so deep, I know there is no place I'd rather be than right here, in Eden. Well, actually just through this gate is where I want to be *most*, but right here is really nice too.

"Are you okay?"

I turn, and Nial is standing a few feet away, his shoulders stiff and his face full of concern. He looks me over from the top of my head to my feet, making sure I'm not hurt, and I get the feeling that even though he's alone out here, he's always this observant and watchful of the people he cares about.

I want to know what has made him choose to be alone when he has so much to give.

I wipe my face and smile at him, feeling touched that I'm included in his consideration.

"I feel at home here," I tell him. I hold my hand out toward the trees on either side of us and lean back against the gate, feeling a charge rush through my body as I do. Much stronger than the buzz seconds ago. My eyes widen and he moves toward me.

"What happened?"

"I don't know! I felt a tenth of that a moment ago, but this was—" I put my fingers together and mimic an explosion. "Electric?" I grin and his worried eyes soften.

"You seem happy," he says, his voice low. "But you've been crying?"

"I *am* happy. This place is...oh! Since you're here with me this time—do you have the secret to opening this gate? I need to see what's over there." I turn to face it again and lean my head against the metal, peering through the wide slats. "It's even more beautiful than here, which doesn't seem possible, but just look!"

He moves next to me, my shoulder touching his arm, and I feel the tension in him with this barest contact.

"No, I do not," he says, his voice broken.

I look at him and see his profile as he stares at the other side. I put my hand on his arm and give it a slight shake. "It's okay. It's not the end of the world!" I laugh, and he looks at me with such profound sadness that I stop. "There must be someone who can open it, right?" I rattle the gate and feel another electrical current so strong this time, I jump back, breathing hard.

He reaches out his hand and I take it. "Let's go back to the house," he says.

I nod, stunned from that jolt. I turn back to look at the gate, and it's like I can see the two of us standing right there with Gabriel and Jophiel. I give my head a brisk shake.

But he's here with me now, and I weave my fingers through his. He looks down at me and his shoulders relax. He smiles and everything feels better. Hopeful.

I don't understand anything that's happening here, but strangely, I'm not afraid. I let my head fall back and I take a huge gulp of this air, letting it fill my lungs.

When we get to the house, I throw my arms around his waist and I can tell it startles him, but he laughs and keeps me from stumbling.

"What's that about?" he asks.

"I needed that walk to the gate," I tell him. "I woke up feeling so off, and I just needed to get outside, get recharged." I laugh, shaking my head. "Literally. That gate zapped me good!"

He chuckles and then he takes a step closer and puts his arms around me, gazing down at me. I go breathless. His beautiful face this close, the feeling of his arms around me, it's almost more than I can take.

And then he lowers his head and kisses me. It's so soft at first that I think he's talking himself out of it and going to pull away, but then his lips brush against mine again, and this time it's longer, more intentional. He looks at me, studying my face to make sure I'm okay with it, I guess? And when he comes back in a third time, I lean up on my tiptoes and put my arms around the back of his neck, kissing him with everything in me.

My back arches into him, our bodies melding together as tight as they can go, while he kisses me back. His tongue clashes against mine, our lips and tongues and teeth nipping and licking and sucking, and our hands everywhere all at once. I can't get close enough and he can't either, and he moans into my mouth, the sound shooting desire between my legs. He picks me up and carries me inside, lying me gently on the bed as he leans over me, his mouth never leaving mine.

I tug his shirt over his head and it's as if I'm dumping cold water over him instead. He pulls back and looks at me with alarm, holding his hand out. My mouth opens to ask him what's wrong, but he shakes his head and grabs his shirt, tugging it back on.

"Forgive me," he says, as he hurries out of the room.

CHAPTER SIXTEEN

I try to catch my breath and not just jump to being offended. But what was that? I know he wanted me as much as I wanted him. He kissed me without abandon, like he'd been dying to do that all along. And I honestly don't know how he was capable of stopping.

That kiss was staggering.

I can't believe he stopped.

It'll just get more uncomfortable between the two of us if I don't find him now and talk it out. I don't want to lose the progress I've made with him.

And I want to wipe all doubt out of his mind because I desperately want to kiss him again.

I look through the house and don't find him. I even check outside, but I don't see him anywhere. And then I look everywhere I've already looked... again. I sit on the couch for a while and go to the library, trying to read, but I can't think of anything but the way his mouth felt like it was made for me.

I press my fingers to my lips, losing myself in thought countless times before giving up reading, and I go look for him again.

There's no way he could be too far, right? I don't know where he goes when he needs space, but since he doesn't have a car, it can't be that far.

I venture toward his room one more time and this time, I hear a door open and close, and then it's quiet. I reach out to turn the knob on the door and it nudges open on its own...it must not have been fully closed.

And the sight I see nearly knocks me sideways.

Nial has one hand against the wall, facing me, his eyes squeezed shut as he fists his long, thick hardness, gliding up and down as fast and urgently as he can. I'm transfixed by the sight, my mouth going dry while everywhere else goes wet, and I swallow hard, putting a hand to my mouth to keep from making a sound.

My eyes are focused on his hands and how it's affecting him, and when he swells and groans, my mouth drops, and I almost groan myself. Ropes of milky white cover his stomach and chest and he slows down the motion, jerking into his hand as the aftershocks keep coming. Until he's completely still.

And that's when I look at his eyes again, and he's looking right at me. I gasp and take him in fully, his bare muscular chest, his hair disheveled and sexier than life...and there are two huge white wings on either side of him.

I feel my throat close, my mouth opening and shutting, but no words and no air are coming out. He steps toward me, reaching down at the last second to grab his shirt and wipe his hand and stomach before he tosses it aside and stands in front of me.

"Phina?" he says softly.

It draws me back, jarring me enough to take a huge inhale and exhale.

"The wings are real," I finally say. "I thought they were just part of the dream nonsense."

"Not nonsense at all," he says.

"Uh, no. I-I see that. Where have those been all this time?"

"I have shielded your eyes from seeing them."

His wings shimmer in the light, the reflection of the sunlight creating a glow so beautiful, I stand in awe. I lower my head to him, and he blinks, lowering his head in response.

That catches me off guard almost more than the fact that Nial has wings, the reverence he returns to me. But I will ponder that later. For now, I reach out and run my fingers along the edge of his wings, enjoying the softness of his feathers and then going inward, along an almost translucent vein of the thinnest skin.

He moans, his teeth sinking over his bottom lip as he takes a shuddering breath, and I can tell it takes effort for him to show restraint.

I lower my hand, despite wishing I never had to stop, knowing I need answers and that I can't let anything distract me this time. Not Nial, this house, the garden, not even his beautiful wings...

"Please tell me," I whisper.

"You still do not fully remember, do you?"

I shake my head. "You're not angry?"

"Why would I be angry?" He sounds truly confused, and I shake my head slowly.

I'm the confused one.

"I honestly never know how you're going to react about...anything," I admit. "You left in a rush and didn't seem happy in my room earlier."

"I was very happy," he says. In complete monotone, no less.

"Huh, interesting. Why did you leave?"

"*That's* what you want to know when you have just seen that I have wings?" He looks away, but he's smiling, and he looks lighter, younger. Free.

I laugh. "I'm blaming every bizarre thing I do and say and think on the fact that I survived a plane crash, suffered a head injury, and...also, whatever happened on that little trip we took. I can't explain what's happening to me. One minute I feel rational, and the next, I believe that I'm getting energy from the garden."

His eyes shoot to mine. "You've realized that?"

"Today when I was outside, it was almost a complete turnaround from how I felt when I woke up. And more than just feeling better after a walk in fresh air."

He nods. "You're more sensitive to it now, and especially after I took you out of the garden. Your reaction to leaving was extreme."

"Why is that?"

"Your body has not fully...acclimated to being here," he says carefully.

"What are you not saying?" I sigh.

"I'm so glad things are coming back to you, Phina. That is how it should be. You coming to your own realizations, not being swayed by what I say and do. Which is why I left your room earlier."

"You're not swaying me," I argue.

"I don't want to take advantage of you while you're healing," he says briskly. Almost like he's rehearsed that response.

"It's not taking advantage when I'm kissing you back. I think maybe I'm even the one who started it earlier? I don't know, but you definitely did *not* take advantage of me."

"It would be easy for you to get attached to me since we're the only two people here, and you haven't regained your full memory yet," he says.

My eyes slide down his body of their own will, landing on the most exquisite erection ever. I swallow hard, forcing my eyes up. It takes an immense level of self-control.

"I don't see the harm in any of that," I say. "And you don't seem to be too uncomfortable with it either since you're still standing here with that—"

I point at him, and my mouth drops again when he closes his fist around his hardness and squeezes. I think I squeak, but I'm not sure. Might have been closer to a whimper.

His eyes are lit from behind, an extra gleam of *something*. Self-confidence, or lust, or amusement. I'm not sure what it is—maybe the sheer fact that I have seen him for who he truly is.

I step toward him, and it's as if he's daring me to come the rest of the way.

I stop when my feet bump his, and I put my hands on his chest, feeling it rise and fall beneath my touch.

"You're not running from me now," I whisper.

"Phina, don't you know by now that I will never run from you?"

I feel like the wind is knocked out of me when he says that, and yet, I try to make light of it. "It seems like I've made you run quite often, now that I think about it."

"Mostly so I didn't do something like this." He points between us at the beautiful body part I'm trying so hard not to look at right now. "And scare you off. Or so these wouldn't come out at the wrong moment." He points at his wings. "And scare you off."

I stare at him for a few long seconds, and he takes a deep breath and turns, walking to the bathroom. I admire the view, sad when he's out of sight. His body is something to behold. I can hardly look away from the wings...they are stunning. But so are his muscular arms and firm cheeks, his thick, muscled legs.

He comes back a few seconds later and has a T-shirt and sweats on. He smells like soap, and I try to hide my disappointment that he's covered up. At least his wings are still out, and I'm glad he isn't trying to hide them from me anymore. Their presence comforts me somehow.

I get a sharp pain in my shoulder blades and reach back, trying to rub the ache away, one shoulder at a time.

CHAPTER
SEVENTEEN

"So, you're an angel," I finally say, knowing he refuses to spell it out for me, and I seem to need it to be spelled out since my mind is still hanging on to the muddled parts of memory that only believe in the human realm. And I can barely wrap my head around that right now, so this is really doing a number on me. "And this place we're in, Eden...is actually...*Eden*." My eyes widen with emphasis on that name. "Why did that not seem significant to me before now?"

I've heard the stories about the Garden of Eden. Now I wish I could remember where I learned about Adam and Eve and the serpent, the apple. The banishment of the first two people from the garden. How some blame Eve for all of it even though Adam had been instructed not to eat the apple and the serpent deceived Eve...which in my mind has always meant that Adam knew exactly what he was doing when he ate the apple, and Eve was tricked. So why doesn't Adam get any blame?

I've always thought Eve got a bad rap, if this is even a true story. And when I try to remember how I felt about it before, it feels right that I felt it was a bit too outlandish and fantastical to really be true.

But Nial has *wings*. I stare at them again, my fascination with them bordering on rude.

And what was that current I felt flowing into me from the gate?

Where do I fit in all of this?

"I just don't understand," I finally say.

"I tell you what, how about let's pause this conversation for now. This has been a lot to take in. Your memory is returning, and the rest will come. You're still recovering, and I don't want you to tire yourself. Are you hungry? I'd like to prepare a few dishes for you, things I know you'll love," he says, smiling.

"Well, when you put it that way, sure." I shrug, but I'm smiling too. "But I feel much better...and just on the edge of—" I shake my head, frustrated that I still have so many blank spaces in my memory. I almost wonder if it would be better if I just went to sleep and let the dreams take over. But that doesn't make sense either, trying to live in a fantasy world that doesn't exist.

And yet, here I am.

And Nial has wings.

He takes my hand, and we walk out of his room, down the long hallway with beautiful rooms, and into the kitchen. He pulls out things I didn't even notice in the refrigerator earlier and begins chopping and marinating.

"What can I do to help?" I ask.

He points at the bottle of wine and the stool next to the island. "Pour us a glass of that and relax?"

"How about I do the salad when that's closer to being done," I offer when he puts a large baking dish in the oven.

He looks at me and beams, which makes my heart do a flip. He hums while he works on the dessert, smiling as he squeezes lemons and makes the cream cheese light and fluffy before adding it to another batter.

I wish I'd known seeing his wings would bring out this side of him.

We talk and sip our wine, and I work on the salad as he puts the cake in the lower oven. I chop everything into small pieces and then work on the dressing, taking a bottle of this and that out of his refrigerator and bar. I feel Nial's eyes on me as I mix seasonings and wine and pour the light vinaigrette over the greens.

He smiles when I look up and pulls two plates out of the cabinet, setting them on the table. He lights the candlesticks and then begins carrying the food to the table. I bring the salad over and admire the fresh blooms he's arranged in a small vase.

He pulls my seat out for me and frowns, glancing at my dress. "I'll be right back. Dig in. Don't wait for me."

And he's off before I can say a word.

I pile my plate with all the delicious food, closing my eyes as the rich aroma fills my senses. When I open them, Nial is taking his seat across from me, and he's wearing a fitted grey shirt and pants and a floral tie with a trinity knot. His wings are tucked behind him, closer to his back, and in the candlelight, they illuminate.

I smile appreciatively and his cheeks flush slightly.

We begin eating and I exclaim over everything I taste, the food so much more flavorful even than yesterday. "How did you learn to cook this way?" I ask.

"Someone I love taught me everything I know in the kitchen," he says, smiling down at his plate.

A bolt of jealousy hits me, and I grip my napkin in my fists. When his eyes meet mine, they're amused, and I glare at him. He chuckles and leans in, his eyes twinkling.

"I made these things especially for you. I thought you'd appreciate them as much as you did the lemon cake."

"You thought right. Best things I've ever tasted. Good call."

He smirks, that look he gets like he knows something I don't, and I want to shake it out of him. Everything I'm missing.

It's as if there's a shroud of mist in my brain, where I think I can almost see through it one second, only to be in the dark the next.

"I'd love to hear you play again, if you feel up to it later," he says, picking up our plates and setting them near the sink before replacing them with a smaller dessert plate. My mouth is already watering as I see him set two dessert options on the table. One is the lemon cake, and the other is a chocolate raspberry cheesecake.

"I can't pick one," I tell him, and he places one of each on my plate.

The flavors are out of this world, and if I were alone, I'd lick the plate clean. He looks so pleased, and I thank him again for the delicious meal.

"I can play for you." I hesitate before adding, "I'm not sure how that happened really. I just sat down and knew what to do."

"Then it will come back to you again," he says.

He does something with his hand then, as we stand up, and the table clears, not a crumb or dish in sight.

My mouth drops and he looks at me, alarmed.

"I-I'm getting too comfortable," he says.

"I don't know why I'm surprised that you can do that." My eyes narrow. "And here I thought you kept things spectacularly clean."

He laughs and something in my chest loosens, a warm feeling washing over me. "It's rare that I rush the cleaning. When I'm alone, it gives me something to do."

He sobers, and I'm struck by the wistful look on his face.

"Why are you out here all alone, Nial?" I ask softly.

"But I'm not anymore," he says just as softly. "You're here."

CHAPTER EIGHTEEN

We go to the music room, and I walk to the harp, unsure of what will happen. But again, once I position the instrument, my hands move into place, and the melodies that flow are beautiful but poignant. I'm near tears by the time the song is done, and I jump up and move to the piano, the need for a happier song making me move quickly.

I sit down and play something lively, periodically wiping my cheeks as tears spill over from the last piece. When I finish playing, I feel better and turn, startled, when Nial claps behind me.

"This house has missed the music…and so have I," he says. He holds out his hand and I take it, and he pulls me up and against his chest as he begins spinning us around the room. Music fills the room, and I wouldn't have thought I knew these dances, but it comes as naturally to me as playing the instruments, as if the very room is weaving magic between us.

We dance until I am dizzy and alive with passion. Every nerve ending in my body is aware of Nial, my body taut and primed for every touch. I feel like I might combust if I don't have him, and as we move in sync, I try to maintain my cool, but inside, I'm unraveling.

When he twirls me dozens of times and then draws me against his chest, I put my hands in his hair and he doesn't disappoint. He lowers his mouth to mine and kisses me like he's as starved for me as I am for him.

We stand still, but I feel like I'm still spinning, the current between us building until I tremble against him. He clutches me tighter and then puts his hands beneath my thighs and lifts me. I wrap my legs around his waist, the long slit in my dress parting the material and showing my skin. He glances down and hisses a breath between his teeth, and I look down. I try to cover myself, heat flaming my face, as the lower half of my body is bare before him, and he shakes his head.

"Do not cover yourself with me, Phina." He kisses me gently this time, but his thumb goes straight for that perfect spot between my legs, and he just barely presses, but it's enough to make me cry out, all inhibition falling by the wayside. A small buzz circulates between us, and his thumb moves faster and faster. I buck against him, and he backs me into the wall where he can get to me even better. His icy heat crackles against my skin, leaving me feeling things in places I've never felt them.

He leans back, my legs still wrapped tightly around him, and dives his fingers inside, his thumb still managing to work me over, and I fall apart in his arms. He catches my cries with his kiss, his fingers moving languidly as I ride it out against him.

"You are the most beautiful creature," he whispers. "So perfect in every way."

I open my eyes and his whole body is shining. I pull his face back to mine and kiss him, before whispering, "Don't stop."

He grins against my lips. "Sweet Phina, so impatient."

I'm afraid if we leave this room, he'll snap out of whatever mood this room is creating, so I start loosening his tie right there. He surprises me by turning and leaving the room, and I tug his face to look at me, to please not let this moment go, and he doesn't. He takes us to the bedroom that I fell in love with, the most beautiful one, and he lowers me reverently onto the bed. I sink into the plush linens and gaze up at him, feeling drunk.

I don't want to know what has changed his mind, why he's okay with this now when he wasn't before. I think he knows what's happening is bigger than both of us. Still, he hesitates as he stands there staring at me.

"Please don't deny me, Nial," I whisper.

That seems to settle it for him. He undoes his tie and unbuttons his shirt. I lean up and undo his pants, and when his shirt is off, he takes my dress off, standing back up and looking down at me in awe.

"I don't know how you could be any more beautiful than this moment, right here, right now," he says.

"You're the most beautiful man I've ever seen," I tell him. "*Angel*," I whisper.

His cheeks flush and when he leans over me, not letting any part of us touch except our mouths, my impatience takes over. I pull him on top of me and he laughs, but he doesn't fight it.

"I've wanted this for so long, I can't believe it's finally happening," he says, leaning up on his elbows, both hands on my face.

I feel his tip against my entrance and tilt my hips up, groaning as he slides in slightly. He backs up and I gasp again, already missing him.

"Should we be careful of—" he starts. "I don't know how it will work with you in this half...I'm not saying any of this right."

"Oh! I wasn't thinking. Condoms." I crinkle my face. That word feels strange here. "Is that right?"

"I believe so," he says. He shakes his hand and holds a foil packet up. "Does this look right?"

I nod. "I think so." I feel as confused as he looks, and I giggle. He opens the packet and frowns when he sees the circle. But he gives a slight shrug and slides it on.

"Interesting," he says. "Okay, where was I?" He grins and lifts my thigh over his, and then kisses me madly as he works his way inside. He makes it excruciating—dipping in just enough to make me want more and then sliding out, the wetness he's creating in me making sounds that he seems to love. I'm embarrassed at first by the sound of my desire, but it just seems to spur him on, his pupils dilating, and he starts moving faster and deeper, until I finally have him right where I want him. When he pulls out and drives back in with one long, hard thrust, I cry out, my back arching, and he doesn't withhold for another second.

He pounds into me relentlessly, and I lean up on my elbows, my hips moving frantically to meet him, and he moves his fingers between my legs again, and it's like a vibration against my skin.

Faster than what is humanly possible, and it sets me off in a violent wave that seems unending.

I scream his name, as wave after wave convulses inside of me, and when I start to be able to think clearly again, I open my eyes and rock furiously against him, reaching up to trace my fingers over the glowing vein in his wings.

"Phina," he says hoarsely. "Oh, my love," he whispers, his head dropping to my neck, as he swells inside of me, and I round off into another explosion against him. "You are made for me. Forever made for me."

I clutch his neck, my hands sliding into his hair, our bodies slick with sweat, and it's as if a thousand memories hit me at once. Us making love in this bed—when we're as young as before and also when we're older—in the poppy fields, the sunflower fields, frequently back in the almond trees lying on mounds of blossoms like that first time, and all over this house and the garden just outside these walls, as well as the more beautiful garden beyond the gate.

I gasp and his eyes widen and then fill with tears. Mine blur too with the emotion, and I whisper, "I remember."

CHAPTER NINETEEN
NIAL

I lower my forehead to hers, my heart threatening to climb into hers, it's pounding so hard.

"Is it really true?" I ask. "Do you really remember?"

"I remember us," she says. "All the pieces haven't come back, but I see us, Nial. Here in this bed, many times. All over the gardens. I see us. We were so happy."

I nod, blinking rapidly, trying to hold it together. "Yes," I whisper.

"How is this possible?" she asks.

"I believe we've been given another chance," I tell her. "I'm not sure why, but I'm just so grateful for it that I haven't tried to find many answers." I'm scared to look too closely for answers, but I don't tell her that part. I don't want to do anything to ruin this moment.

"There's still so much I don't understand, but it's coming back to me, right?" she says hopefully.

I trace my fingers down her cheek and over her full lips. "If you remember us, that's all I could hope for. And you're right, we've spent countless hours doing this right here, in this bed."

She squirms when I press into her again, and I remember that I have that odd contraption on. We never used those before, but I wanted to be respectful of her human form and not give her a baby before she's ready for one, mentally or physically.

I pull out slowly and her teeth bite into her lower lip as she frowns.

"Am I hurting you?" I ask.

"I'm surprised you didn't with that massive sword you have." She laughs and so do I, stunned when she brings back a memory from our first time. "You've grown even larger than I remember."

"I'm sure it's just from the lack of us," I tease. "And I'm considerably older than the last time you saw me, so I suppose my body has matured too."

"Am I different than before?"

"You are the same and more. There might be much that I do not know about you now, much that I've missed, but perhaps I know more than you'd think. You are still *you*, the one I will love throughout eternity."

Her eyes fill and I lean in, kissing her tears away. "When can you tell me everything?" she asks.

"I still cannot," I tell her sadly. "But I trust now that your memories will return."

She looks slightly troubled when I lift off of her and I kiss her again, smoothing the space between her brows.

"Do not fret," I whisper.

I go to dispose of the condom and when I crawl back into our bed, I smile when I see that she's fallen asleep. I lift her hand and weave my fingers through hers, lifting her hand to my lips.

"Sweet dreams, my Phina. Thank you for coming back to me. You have exceeded all I could ever hope for."

Her body shudders and her brow creases again, and I lean over and kiss her forehead.

"Shh, it's okay."

When she does it again, I'm tempted to wake her up, but so far, her dreams have been helpful in leading her to more answers, even if she's not always realized it. But she tosses and turns, and I lift her toward me, pressing her chest against mine, as I wrap my arms around her. I whisper how much I love her, my heart so full of gratitude, and tears stream down my face that we've been given this chance.

She cries out and I rub her back, massaging the area where I know her phantom wings are causing her pain, and hope it won't be long before she remembers everything, so she won't have to suffer with this any longer.

She shakes her head. "No," she cries. "No."

"Phina?" I try to wake her this time. If she's dreaming about the plane crash, I want to save her that torment. "Wake up, my love."

She shudders again and then sits straight up. I sit up next to her, my hand tentatively reaching for her. I don't want to startle her. She turns to face me and says, "He's coming," with sheer terror in her voice.

My blood runs cold. I haven't wanted to believe he would dare show his face around us again, but I should've known better.

If what she's saying is true, I should reach out to the five. I lost them when I lost her, and while it hasn't been to the same degree as it's been with her, I've still missed them every day. I'm not sure if they'll respond to my call, but I must try.

They know she's here, that much I'm sure of. What I don't know is whether we'll be banished even further if we try to be together. I can only hope it's a good sign that no attempts to interfere have been made before now.

Phina lies back, her eyes closed again, and she sleeps soundly for a while. When she wakes, she stretches and presses her lips against my chest, making me stir to life again.

Well, I've been stirred all along with her lying next to me, but this time, I do something about it. She sits up, straddling me, and I sit up too, pulling her down on me with one long thrust. Her head falls back, and I sink my head into her tits, worshipping her the way I've wanted to for so long.

It's not until afterward that I remember I didn't use the rubber barrier and I hurriedly wave my hand over her womb, removing all parts of me that could try to linger and create a baby. I should've just done that the first time instead of producing something out of thin air.

She sighs into my arms again, falling into another deep slumber, and I decide to let all worry go for this one night. We can deal with whatever madness may come...tomorrow.

CHAPTER TWENTY

The night is the most amazing, endless repeat of wake, love, and sleep. I don't know how many times we repeat the cycle, but I sleep just long enough to get the stamina to explore his body and then do that all over again. When I wake up and the sun is shining through the windows, my body is sated and I feel so good, so *alive*.

Every time I woke up in the night, Nial was awake, but now he sleeps, and as much as I want to wake him and melt into his body, I want him to rest.

His eyes pop open and he smiles at me.

"I'm sorry I woke you," I say, leaning my chin on his chest.

"I was not asleep. Just closing my eyes, trying to distract myself from your body," he says, laughing.

"Do you not need sleep?" I ask.

He shakes his head. "There are times my body needs the rest, but even then, it's not quite sleeping. More like a stillness, a time to ruminate."

"It must have made the night feel long, having me sleep so often."

"The night flew faster than my wings do." He kisses my forehead, moving my hair away from my elbow so I don't pull the long strands lying on his chest. "How do you feel today?" He studies me carefully, his expression slightly anxious.

I smile and shake my head, my eyes rolling up to the ceiling. "So good I can't even tell you. I don't remember seeing colors so crisp or my body feeling so vibrant." I lower my face, kissing his chest as my cheeks flush. "And I feel all the places you've been, inside and out. It's like a cool burn, flames licking throughout my body with an icy tongue."

His eyes heat and he pulls me against him, his wings cocooning us in a shimmering white glow. "You felt that, huh? I wasn't sure if—"

"Wait, so that's something you actually did inside me?" I whisper the last words, my face heating more.

He smirks and I feel the rush now throughout my body, as that feeling builds inside of me, from my chest and my heart beneath, down my stomach, and then letting a glacial inferno loose between my legs and inside of me, as he lies there innocently staring at me.

My mouth parts and I quiver and quake without him laying a finger on me. In seconds, no less.

He's hard as a rock, and I try to focus on the flames still flicking in and out of me, imagining them lighting up his legs and circling throughout his body until he can't help but explode.

His eyes widen and I can tell he's trying to hold back, but I don't let go, not when I've just discovered what I'm capable of.

He drags me on top of him and pushes into me, and when those raging fires are combined, the result is explosive. I have an out-of-body experience, the pleasure almost too much. And then there's pressure in my shoulder blades. It's not pain this time though, the rapturous feeling making my entire body tremble inside and out.

"Phina," Nial's voice rasps.

The combination of what Nial is doing inside of me and his voice saying my name like I'm everything to him makes me fall apart. I shatter into a million pieces and then gasp as my wings extend. Nial looks at me in awe, and the edges of my wings that brush against Nial's create spasm after spasm in both of us.

"I love you," I cry, and the very ground shakes beneath us.

"For a thousand lifetimes," he says, clutching either side of my face.

"And beyond."

There's a booming rumble outside, a gust of wind that reminds me of the ocean, and Nial and I stare at each other in shock.

"Wow," I whisper, laughing. My head drops to his chest, and unlike the other times we've been together, I don't feel tired at all.

"You look like you're about to bounce out of your skin," Nial says. "Come on, let's go outside."

We crawl out of the bed, not bothering with putting on clothes, and walk out of the glass doors. He turns to face me, his hands on my waist. One hand reaches up to tease my nipple too, and I grin, pretending to swat him away.

"Are you ready?" he asks.

My mouth parts. "Am I?"

"Yes."

He sounds surer than I feel, but I trust him, so I handle it about the same as I did the harp. I do what comes naturally, shooting straight up until I'm over the trees, and then extending my wings and soaring through the sky. I laugh and squeal and feel topsy-turvy at times, but when I glance at Nial flying next to me, the elation on his face, I know that I'm doing it. This is no dream.

"I'm flying," I yell. "Can you believe I'm flying?" I laugh when I realize how crazy I sound. Of course, he believes it—he's seen me do it, and even though I am beginning to remember it like the back of my hand, my times in the sky, it still feels like it's been far too long.

How did I survive without this?

Without him?

We fly over the places I've walked, and I'm tempted to see if we can fly by the site of the accident, mostly curious if I'll feel any weakness now that I have my wings. But it's too soon. I want to enjoy this time with Nial, every single moment.

CHAPTER
TWENTY-ONE

Since time is so unusual here, I think about it less and less. But we must spend the equivalent of a week or two or three in bed, maybe six, only leaving it to eat and bathe and fly. The memories I have of us together are exquisite, even though I know there's something that came between us, something so big, I'm scared to face it. *Terrified*.

But despite how happy I know we were, I don't remember being *this* happy. Knowing that despite huge obstacles that are still beyond my understanding, we are being given another chance...it's the absolute best feeling I can imagine.

Nial doesn't say much about his time without me, but I know by how happy he is now too, that he must have been so lonely without me. That's the only thing that sometimes falters my utter joy—the thought of him alone. I've stopped asking him to tell me details because it seems to upset him when he can't answer me, and he's right—it will come. I have to believe the whole truth will be revealed when it's time.

We decide to get outside for a bit and venture to the waterfall. I splash him and chase him or swim away as he chases me, loving when he catches me. I'll never get tired of how his arms feel around me, his skin against mine, our wings touching. But I back up from him suddenly, standing up in the water and turning to him in horror.

"What is it?" he asks, rushing to my side.

"I just got a horrible feeling. I don't know how to explain it."

He looks worried and bites the inside of his cheek. "Did you see something? Someone?"

"No." I put my hand on my throat and then my stomach. "It was more of a sick feeling."

He nods slightly and looks up at the sky. "I was afraid of this," he says softly.

"You know what's happening?"

"I have a good idea. I should've reached out to

the others before now. I just didn't want to...miss a moment with you. I've been selfish."

I place my hand on his chest, his heart, and love the feel of it pounding against me. "I'm not going anywhere," I tell him.

He doesn't say anything, and that's unsettling in itself. He's still, on alert, and it's a while before he turns to me. "Why don't we get inside? Are you still feeling strange?"

He steps out of the water and holds his hand out for me to take. I take it and walk toward him, his eyes on my body making me shiver. He puts his arm around me, and I warm instantly, as we walk to the house.

"Who are the others?" I ask.

"I should send word and see if they come before I get your hopes up unnecessarily."

"Because I'll be excited when I see them?"

"I believe you will, if you remember them."

When we step into the house, I breathe a little easier, but those uneasy feelings stick with me throughout the rest of the day. Nial spends time in the library and doesn't make me feel like I shouldn't be in there, but I want to give him privacy for however he plans to correspond with his friends. I almost ask him how he sends word when there's no phone, and I suspect not typically a laptop since it disappeared after that day I used it.

The longer I'm here, the more removed I feel from those things.

Since I don't remember friends from my life before the crash, I don't feel any urgency to wonder who or what else I might be missing. Because here, with Nial, I'm not missing a thing.

By the waterfall earlier felt similar to how I felt when we visited the crash site, although fainter than that. The longer I'm inside though, losing myself in playing piano and singing softly while Nial is busy, the more I second-guess those feelings. Maybe we've been spending too much time inside and it was just an overload of all the goodness—the sun, the water, Nial. I stop trying to figure it out and close my eyes, letting the music soothe my thoughts.

I feel his hands on my back later and smile, sinking back into him.

"I love to hear your music in this house," he says. "I've missed the way you—"

He starts sentences like that often and doesn't finish. I've learned to not be bothered by it because he tells me so much in the things he does say, the way he reveres my body, the man he reveals to me more every day...

"Did you reach your friends?" I ask.

"It's not as simple as that, but I did what I could."

I turn to face him, and he looks down at me with concern. "How are you feeling?"

"Absolutely fine. I've chalked it up to needing to get outside more." I laugh, my hands wrapping around his waist as I lean forward and plant kisses on his stomach, making sure to get each dip in every sculpted ab. His muscles twitch underneath my touch, his instant hardness tenting under his pants.

I undo the button and zipper of his linen pants and wrap my hands around him, my tongue swirling over his tip, so light, but I know in the way his knees buckle that he feels everything. I tease and lick and flick his tip until I know he's dying to tug my hair and thrust down my throat, but I want to make him wait.

He groans, and as I stare up at him, his pupils dilate, his eyes looking darker and a bit feral. I hum, loving the taste of him, loving the heady power that comes with making him lose control.

When his whole body is taut with restraint, only then do I take him in as far as I can, bobbing my head slowly up and down, and then back to the shallow flick of my tongue.

I look up at him and he swallows hard. "Don't be careful with me," I tell him. I open my mouth wider to accommodate more of him and clutch his firm cheeks with my hands, sliding him in and out of my mouth until he takes over and starts thrusting. He's a true vision then, his head thrown back when he's not looking at me, eyes fierce, and driving into me with abandon.

I moan around him, loving every minute of this, and he goes deeper. My eyes roll back when he does that thing inside of me, the icy fire that licks me all over and then settles between my legs, making me see stars. It's a good thing he's taken over because I can't concentrate on making him feel good anymore—he's making me lose my mind. But he goes faster and faster and my mouth takes it, as we both collide into frenzied pleasure. I take every drop as he continues pumping into me, and then he pulls out, picking me up, and drives into my wet heat, somehow already ready for more.

"Nial," I chant, shaking my head back and forth, bouncing up and down, both of us slick from desire. And when we both fall over the edge together this time, the house shakes and shudders around us.

CHAPTER TWENTY-TWO

We start cooking together, and I realize I'm quite good in the kitchen. As I watch him prepare things, it feels familiar, and now that I'm more comfortable here, it's like things just come to me easier. I don't know if it's things I was good at before, or if this actual place brings out the best in me. Perhaps both.

But Nial loves it that I'm cooking now and enjoying it, and when I begin making him things, surprising him with new dishes I try, you'd think it was the best thing he'd ever tasted.

"It tastes better when you make it," he says. "Everything does."

"You're just tired of cooking," I tease.

He laughs. "Not true. If we wanted, we could snap our fingers and there would be food here." His eyes widen and he looks like he's told me something he shouldn't have yet again. I have a hard time keeping up with what's off-limits and just laugh it off.

I snap my fingers and lemon cake appears. I clap my hands, delighted. "That's amazing!"

He laughs, shaking his head. "But where is the joy in the preparing when you simply wave a hand or snap a finger?"

"The joy is in having more time to do this," I say, my arms around him as I leap up, my legs wrapping around his waist. His hands rest on my backside and he grins, leaning in to kiss me.

"I do approve of all the time we can do this," he says.

I kiss him and then pull back, my hands tugging on his hair...one of my many favorite parts of him. "I think I may take a walk today, make you miss me...*and* to look for ingredients for a surprise I have for you."

His head tilts, his lips lifting in a smile. I love how much he smiles now. "What kind of surprise?"

"No, no. You're not the only one who can have

secrets." I laugh when he tickles my side. "It's about time that I have something up my sleeve."

"You and these funny expressions," he says, chuckling. He holds out my arm and drags his tongue along my skin. "There is no sleeve to be found."

I giggle, pulling his head between my breasts, where he gets lost for a while.

By the time I finally get outside, he's had me in three different positions, not counting the last time in the shower. I'm in full bliss mode, barely remembering the berries I wanted to look for to try in a recipe. I decide as long as I'm out here, I'll enjoy a walk to the gate and then I'll pick the berries on my way back. I practice shielding my wings, something Nial taught me to do recently, so I won't be tempted to fly instead of walking.

It's been so long now since we've done anything apart, that I'm already missing Nial before I've even gotten halfway. I laugh out loud.

"You have got it so bad," I say under my breath.

When I reach the gate, something feels different right away. I look up when a gust of wind fills the air, the trees and flowers whipping around with the sudden breeze.

And then my stomach drops to the ground when I hear a deep voice behind me say, "Hello, Sera."

I turn and a blond man is standing there,

leaning against the gate a few feet away. His eyes are so dark it's hard to tell if they're brown or just mostly pupils. He's tall, but a few inches shorter than Nial, and he smiles at me in a way that says he knows me.

He's familiar and yet *not*.

He moves toward me, and I freeze, unsure of what to do, especially when he puts his arms around me and hugs me. I pat his back awkwardly, hoping it'll come back to me who he is.

He leans his head back, keeping me in place with his arms.

"I'm so glad you're okay," he says. "You look beautiful." He leans his forehead against mine and frowns when I pull away. "Sera?"

"Are you one of Nial's friends?" I ask, my voice shaky.

I look around wildly, wondering if there's anything I can do to get Nial out here. We've never talked about that—there hasn't been the need for it since we've been together nonstop.

A tiny crease forms between his brows. He's quite handsome and seems comfortable here. "Hadraniel?" he says, his voice gruff.

That's when I begin to consider that he's not someone Nial contacted, and I wonder what he would be doing all the way in Eden.

"Were you hurt badly from the crash?" he asks.

I take a deep breath. "Oh, you know about the

crash," I say, relieved. He must be one of Nial's friends after all.

"Know about it? I survived it too." His mouth is grim as I gape at him. "Sera, do you know who I am?"

"Are you—"

"Dane," he answers, as if I should know.

I study his features and...there was the faint memory of a blond man I had when I first got here. I could never see him very clearly, but this must be him. I *was* traveling with someone.

"I'm sorry. I suffered an extreme head injury. My memory is taking a while to fully return." My hands twist behind my back. *Nial. I need you.*

"We are the only two survivors," Dane says.

"I thought I was the only one," I say weakly.

He lets out a laugh that sounds harsh and I shiver, wrapping my arms around myself. He takes a step closer, his face contrite.

"It's not your fault, baby. You were hurt," he says, his voice low and seductive.

I see us standing near a bed together, in a sparse apartment full of dark furniture I don't like. He's thrusting into me from behind, my body thicker than it is now, his face less chiseled too. I look back at him over my shoulder and he tugs my hair, pounding into me harder.

Shame fills me. How could I do that to Nial? How is any of this possible? And yet, if he's the one

I was with when I had the plane crash, is he the one I should be feeling guilty for betraying now?

Dane grins at me, his teeth extra white and his canine teeth longer than his incisors. His eyes roam across my face and down my neck, settling on the cleavage that this dress is highlighting. I'm sure my cheeks are flushed, and my breaths are shallow and raspy, which he seems to think is a reaction to him because he licks his lips and leans in like he's about to kiss me.

I'm on the verge of panic, and then I hear Nial's voice.

"Phina," he calls.

"Nial," I gasp.

Dane and I turn, and Nial swoops down, his wings fully extended. He looks formidable, and I expect Dane to cower when he sees a man with wings, but he takes a step closer to me and puts his arm around my shoulder.

Nial looks at me with an unreadable expression and I try to think of something to say, but I'm at a complete loss.

"Dagon," Nial spits out. "You have a lot of nerve showing your face here."

Chapter Twenty-Three

Nial

I heard her say she needed me and the panic that lit through me was enough to send me toppling through the sky in my hurry to reach her. I'd been talking with Raphael for the first time in so long, I was off my game. Unattuned to the shift in the air until it was too late.

When I see him standing next to her, *touching her*, the fury is all-consuming. I see him as he really is, a shriveled, hairless, hideous creature that's missing teeth, and what teeth he does have are gnarly and brown. But I'm certain Phina can't see past his shield, not yet. To her, he's showing something altogether different.

Something bright and shiny and beautiful.

The architect of lies.

"You let her believe I was dead?" he sneers.

Phina looks at me, eyes widening, and then at him, her lips parting as she turns back to me, shaking her head. "You *knew* Dane was with me on the plane?" Her voice is full of horror and disbelief.

"He not only let you believe I was dead—he's the one who caused the crash," Dagon says.

"Silence, Dagon," I yell. I have to be careful of what I say if I hope to keep Phina with me, and Dagon knows that. He's been using it against me since the day we were banished.

"Is that true?" Phina asks. She looks so betrayed, it takes everything in me to not rush toward her and take her in my arms. Kiss her until she remembers that she knows me, knows my heart.

"Dagon is incapable of telling the truth," I tell her, hoping if she never believes another word I say, that this is something that sinks in and resonates.

"Why do you call him that? His name is Dane," Phina says.

Dagon bares his teeth at me. "That's right." He pats her shoulders and smiles sweetly at her, and she seems to buy it.

I get that sick feeling in my stomach that she mentioned having the last time we swam in the waterfall. Dagon must have been lurking in the air then. And with the things Dagon set in motion when he crashed that plane, evil incarnate, the barriers that were in place must now be hanging in the balance. Otherwise, I don't see how he gained access here.

Now it's more urgent than ever that I speak to the others. I still don't understand Dagon's motive behind the crash, not when he finally had Phina where he wanted her.

"What do you want?" I ask.

"Once I realized Sera was here, I came to let her know I'm alive and that I'm taking her home."

Her eyes shoot to mine in panic. She shakes her head. "I cannot leave," she says.

He laughs as if she's joking, and she keeps shaking her head.

"But, baby, we have a life together," he says, his voice smooth as silk.

I feel like I'm going to throw up. "She doesn't remember you," I yell. "You need to leave. You're agitating her."

Her eyes fill with tears, and she moves away from him, his hand dropping from her shoulder. "I am so ready to understand what is going on. You two know each other? How is *that* possible?"

Now that she's far enough away from him, I lift my hand and pelt ice toward Dagon, and as I knew they would, his wings extend. She gasps and puts her hand over her mouth. His wings are black, and I narrow my eyes to see them the way she might. I groan inside. What are actually pathetic wings that have rips and burns throughout them, one way smaller and ragged than the other, to *her*, he's showing magnificent thick black feathers lined in gold.

He looks at me with a smirk, and I hover slightly above the ground, ready for whatever he tries to do next.

"Is it true you made me think he was dead? And that you caused the plane crash?"

"No, it's not true," I reply.

Dagon sputters, about to snap at me, when Phina brings out her wings. Dagon stares at her in surprise and then his eyes gleam. He advances toward her, and I fly between them, putting my hand on his chest.

"Do not come one step closer," I tell him.

"You don't have a say in what she decides," he hisses.

"That may be true, but your days of having a say in what she decides are also over. She came back, and what we have cannot be broken."

"That's not how she felt about it when I had my dick inside her," he says.

"Dane!" she cries. We both turn to look at her and her face is red with anger and embarrassment.

"I don't know what's going on here, but I'll find out." Her voice rises with each word. "Without either one of you having a say!"

She takes off, lifting straight up into the sky and then flying toward the house.

Dagon and I watch her until she's out of sight and then turn toward each other.

"I mean it, Dagon. You will not win this time. You should have known better than to bring her within a thousand feet of me."

"I fully intended for her to come back here and experience the full wonders of Eden. So, she had a little lovefest with you while she was here, so what? It will still be my baby she carries when she leaves. Her earthly body was pathetic." He makes a face, and my fist smashes into his nose. He barely registers it, his scrawny shoulders lifting in a shrug. "She needed to come back here and get her angelic juices flowing again. And then we'll have the most powerful creation that has ever walked the face of the earth."

"Over my dead body," I snarl.

He rubs his hands together, his brown teeth clenched. "Oh, I cannot wait for that day."

CHAPTER TWENTY-FOUR

I go to my room and stumble into the bathroom, rinsing my face with cold water. It's been so long since I've even been in this room. Nial and I have been staying in the big bedroom since we got together. I feel like a stranger again when I look in this mirror, trying to remember how I felt when I got here, how I looked, how I tried to remember who I'd been with and then just let that fall from my mind like a cookie crumb dropping to the ground.

I can't get warm, and I get in the shower and

scrub hard, my body feeling unfamiliar again and dirty and raw. When I get out, I put on the warmest clothes I can find, which is hard to do with all these flowy clothes that are made for the paradise weather that is Eden.

I get under the covers, shifting to my side, and nearly cover my head as I fight through the chills. I replay everything that happened, how furious Nial was, and the way the two of them hate each other. Nial never mentioned Dagon or Dane, whatever his name is, and I would think he'd prepare me if Dane were someone I should be concerned about. Is it jealousy? Did I choose Dane over Nial before? I can't imagine that, but I can't even begin to guess what else it could be.

It seems impossible that I'd ever walk away from what I have with Nial.

As angry and confused as I am with him right now, the thought of leaving is more than I can take. Overwhelmed and jittery, I haven't needed to sleep for a long time, but it's like my body knows I'm maxed out right now. I give in to the sleep and when I begin dreaming, it's different this time. It's as if I'm aware enough to know I could shake myself out of the dream, but I'm too curious to know what memory will come this time.

. . .

I'm crying in a restaurant bathroom, still shaking mad. I didn't even want to come to this work event, but Dane was insistent. He wanted me to impress his colleagues and bought this dress that looks nothing like me. Black and so tight, I feel smothered.

I wipe my tears away and take a deep breath. I can't keep hiding out in this stall, but the last thing I want to do is go back out there when he's practically dry humping Stella, one of his paralegals, on the dance floor.

But that's not what has me worked up the most.

I step outside the stall when I'm sure no one is in the bathroom and glance at my reflection. I lower the material on my dress, looking at the bruises he gave me before we came tonight. He wanted to have sex and I wanted to finish getting ready, so he bent me over the sink and held me by the neck while he forced his way inside.

He's been getting rougher, not ever like this before, but...it's beginning to scare me.

I turn on the cold water and cup my hands underneath, letting them fill and then splashing it on my face. My face is still splotchy, but I take my hair out of the high ponytail and shake it, letting my waves fall forward like a security blanket.

I straighten my shoulders and grab a towel from the bowl on the counter, drying my hands. When I leave the bathroom, he's waiting for me in the hall.

"Baby, you look upset. Come dance with me."

"Go back to Stella. I'm leaving."

He chuckles and then his eyes narrow when he realizes I'm serious. "Don't be ridiculous. Come dance with me." He grabs my arm and I yank it back.

I walk past him, and he moves next to me, hissing under his breath, but trying to outwardly appear like we're fine in front of all his coworkers.

"If you don't get on that fucking dance floor with me in the next two minutes, I'm going to make you regret it for a long time," he says.

I stop walking and turn to face him. "I'll get my things when you're at work. We're done, Dane."

"We're done when I say we're done," he says. His eyes widen when I back away from him, turning around only when I reach the door.

I step out into the cold New York air and breathe deeply. That felt good. Right. I move toward the edge of the sidewalk, and a car comes out of nowhere, knocking me off my feet.

I startle when I feel the bed compress next to me. I open my eyes to find Nial watching me.

"You fell asleep?" he asks with concern.

I'm so unsettled about the dream, I want to tell him everything, but I need to let it sink in first. That was such an awful feeling. Why would I ever go back to him? I search my mind for what came after that, but it's not clear.

"Phina? Are you okay?"

"It felt different than sleeping," I answer. "Something more like a lucid dream but not even that. Almost like I inserted myself into a memory. That person I was before—I had no memory of you." I sit up and put my back on the headboard. "This lack of memories—it's more than a head injury. I was a different person."

He shakes his head but doesn't say anything.

"What? Are you disagreeing?" My voice breaks, and I pull the covers up as far as they'll go, which isn't far enough. "Was I many different people?"

"You have always been you," he says softly.

"Well, that sounds nice in theory, but how old am I, Nial? How old are you?"

"You know I cannot—"

"If you say you cannot answer me one more time, I will scream," I say between gritted teeth. "I don't even know why I came back into this house, other than I don't remember enough to know where to go or how to get out of here." I get out of bed and start pacing. "Things I know were second nature to me before are now hazy, while things like *flying* feel normal. Explain *that* to me. No, you *cannot*," I mimic his low voice and he winces.

"What did you feel when you saw him?" he asks, and I see red.

"I'm not warranting that with a response. You don't get to hold everything to your chest while expecting me to reveal every thought and feeling I have. I'm not playing this game with you anymore." I turn away so I don't have to look at him.

"It's not a game to me, Phina. I thought maybe your response to him would tell you all you need to know, during this time when your memory is not fully there."

I sigh, my shoulders drooping, and the edges of my wings drag on the floor. "I felt confused. Afraid."

"And what did you feel when you first saw me?"

I turn toward him sharply and glare at him.

"This is not for my ego's sake, I swear it." His voice is like melancholy music.

"I thought you were the most beautiful man I'd ever seen. I wanted to lean into your presence."

He's quiet, and I think about what my conflicting feelings between the two could mean.

"It's different though. I haven't seen another person here in all this time. It's normal that I would be frightened."

"Perhaps," he says.

"The thought of you letting all those people die in that crash..." I put my hand over my mouth, but it doesn't keep the sob in.

"You asked me if that was true and I told you it wasn't," he insists, standing up and putting his hands on my shoulders.

I flinch away from him. "I'm sure you can understand why I don't know what to believe right now."

Chapter
Twenty-Five

His eyes are so sorrowful, I almost feel sorry for him. *Almost.*

But a sound in the other room has me turning to him for reassurance.

"He wouldn't just walk into this house, would he?" I whisper. The thought of Dane in the home Nial and I have been sharing together—Nial's personal space, *our safe haven*—feels so wrong.

Nial has an odd expression on his face.

"What?" I whisper.

He breaks out into a huge smile and holds out his hand. I'm so astounded, I take it, and then drop it in the next second. He smirks slightly, which just annoys me more, and we walk down the hall toward the living room.

When we get there, three majestic angels are standing there, chuckling about the sculptures.

"That looks nothing like me," one says.

Nial snorts and they turn as one, their wings tucked into their backs but still impressive. Extremely beautiful men, their countenances shimmer with more of a glow than Nial's...or mine.

They bow their heads, and Nial and I do the same, and when we all raise them again, they're smiling and rush toward us, with their hands outstretched. They're hugging Nial like they haven't seen him in such a long time, and I remember Nial mentioning once that this used to be a meeting place. This must be who the rooms belonged to when they'd meet here. When *we'd* meet here.

I see all of us here, sitting at the long table in the dining room, and in the music room, playing the instruments and singing, dancing.

As soon as I touch his hands, I know it's Michael. His hair is long and white, his eyes a pale blue. He grips my hands firmly and kisses both cheeks, his eyes filling with tears. "How I have missed you, fair one," he says.

A lump fills my throat, and a few tears spill over. "I didn't know how much I'd missed you until now," I whisper. "All of you. But now..." I put my hand on my throat because it suddenly feels like it's on fire. "It's coming back to me."

The others turn and stare at me, and Raphael comes over, barreling into me with a hug. He has dark skin and green eyes and the biggest smile of all of them.

"Welcome back," he says hoarsely.

"Thank you." I laugh when he leans back and studies my face, beaming.

"More beautiful than ever." He drops his hands, and Azrael steps up, smiling at me shyly.

I hold my hand out and he takes it, pulling it to his lips to kiss. His long blond hair dusts my hand, and his dark blue eyes are smiling when he looks at me again.

"I'm so glad you returned," Azrael says quietly. "We can be complete again."

I'm so moved by that, tears run down my cheeks, but I'm laughing as I wipe my face.

"Gabriel and Jophiel will be here later. They're taking care of matters around the borders," Michael says, his attention on Nial. "I'm so glad you reached out when you did. We had sensed activity for a while but didn't realize this was where he was coming in."

Nial looks at them and his face flushes. He looks nervous, and I wonder why, when he begins to speak. "Since we're all here together—well, except for Gabriel and Jophiel, but I can repeat it to them later—I would like to make it known to all of you that I have spent the past thousand plus years missing you so deeply. I've had all the time in the world to think about what I've done, and I will never, ever abandon my duty to you again...if you, and the Almighty sees fit to let me serve with you again. Now that Phina is back, I think maybe we've both been given a second chance."

They all start speaking at once, surrounding him and squeezing his shoulder and head and hands.

"All is forgiven."

"You have more than paid the price."

"If it had been up to us, you never would've been banished."

Banished. That word sticks out and I turn to Nial. "That's why we're here and not beyond the gate..."

He nods once.

"You said we should step away from our duties at the gate, be together...that we worked too hard anyway," I whisper, as it starts to flood back.

"I was wrong. I was so consumed by you. I let it blind me to everything else," he says, moving in front of me.

"But I went with you. I should have said no."

He shakes his head. "It was all my fault. I'd seen Dagon slithering around the day before and ignored him. I didn't realize what he was capable of then. Nothing like that had ever happened in all our time of guarding the gate."

"He was part of the fall," I whisper. "*He's* the one who is to blame. We were given a choice to stay here or to leave, and I couldn't live with the guilt of what I'd done. If I hadn't let the enemy get inside, none of this would have happened. Mankind would be in such a different place..." I think back to my life in New York, how empty I felt there, even while trying to help people and make a difference. "My memories were wiped clean the day I left the garden."

Nial nods, his eyes shining. "That's the day I lost you."

I reach for him, and he wraps his arms around me, hugging me as tight as he can. "I'm back," I whisper. "And I remember everything."

"You are right to say that Dagon is the one responsible," Michael says. "And he's back in our midst, slinking around like he owns the place."

I pull back and Nial wipes my tears away. I lean on my tiptoes and kiss him and then take a step back.

"I was deceived by Dagon," I tell them. "He made me believe he loved me, but we had a tumultuous relationship. I remembered something while I was resting. I think any time I came close to leaving him, he found a way to stop me. Often drastic measures. Was he the one to wipe my memories of Eden?"

They all look at me with various levels of concern. Nial looks like he's about to go off in a fit of rage, but Michael puts his hand on his shoulder, and it has a calming effect.

Michael clears his throat. "I'd assumed it was the Almighty who banished you and took your memories when you left, but...everything was so strange at that time. There were barriers in place that had never been before. We tried to see you many times, Nial, and could never get through... not until now. It makes more sense to think it was evil at work keeping all of us from one another, than the one who has only ever loved us."

"Where is he?" I ask. "Why doesn't he show himself?"

"He's everywhere," Azrael says, smiling. "He's in the waterfall, the beautiful skies, the wind...the air we breathe."

I take a deep breath, knowing he's right, but a little extra backup when danger comes would be nice.

"I'm not sure why Dane's acting like he wants me back. I thought he'd know better than to think anything would ever happen here, but if he got away with it before...maybe that's exactly why he's here now."

"He's counting on you not remembering so he

can swoop in and take you back," Nial says. He glances at Michael. "I hope it's okay that I tell her that much."

"Now that she's remembered who she is, who you are...and Dagon...I think you may speak freely," Michael says. "You're not affecting her choices at this point."

Nial sighs with relief. "You don't know how hard it was to keep this from you all this time," he says to me urgently.

"I'm so sorry I left you," I whisper. "I took it on as my penance." A sob breaks out. "I was crazy to think it was the right thing for anyone." I shake my head and take a deep breath. "Being banished here, with *you*...it would've still been wonderful." I put my head in my hands. "I'm the one who made it torturous for both of us, and you've been so forgiving of *me* all along, taking the blame upon yourself." I put my hands on his cheeks. "I don't know how I will ever deserve you."

"None of us are worthy. It's only love that makes us fit for anything," he says, kissing my wet cheeks.

I take a shuddering breath and laugh, fanning my face. "Okay, I'm sorry, guys, that this has all come back to me right as you're getting here," I tell them. "There have been huge blanks in my memory that just got filled in."

"You just needed to see *us* to have it all come

back," Raphael says. "I've always thought you had a little bit of a crush on me anyway," he teases, lifting an eyebrow. "I'm glad I could bring it all back just like that." He snaps.

I laugh and Nial snorts.

"In your dreams, Raphael," he says, rolling his eyes but laughing. His face quickly turns serious as he turns back to me. "Dagon crashed the plane, Phina. He wants to have a child with you, and his plan wasn't working, so he got you close to Eden, thinking your body would be restored, and you'd have the most powerful child together."

I stare at him, sick to my stomach. "I can't believe I fell for any of his lies, now or then."

"He must be stopped," Nial says. "He got away with turning the world upside down once before. If he gets a foothold inside the gate, I'm not sure what damage he'll do this time."

CHAPTER TWENTY-SIX

"I would love to take him down myself," I say, my blood pumping with rage. "But I know I'm still regaining my strength."

"That's what we're here for," Raphael says. "And if we wait until Gabriel and Jophiel arrive to confront Dagon, our chances are even better of driving him out. Preferably for an eternity this time."

The wind outside howls, and for the first time since I arrived, the skies are grey. When rain starts falling, I'm concerned.

"Is he causing this?" I ask.

Nial nods. "He's just messing with us. A little rain is nothing."

But I'm taken back to the plane dropping out of the sky and landing in the water, that feeling that everything was upside down. And all the times I've been deceived by Dagon, not just in Eden but my life in New York and other lives I've lived all over the world since leaving the garden. He's found me in every one. Now that I know the truth, I see the various forms he's taken to keep me from knowing who he really is.

A man in a subway who tried to win me over and attacked me when I didn't give in. A friendly guy at school who I never gave the time of day, strangling me and ending that life way too soon. A friend's brother who asked me out and the last time I said no, I woke up in the hospital from an unexpected fall and didn't survive the week.

Until he created Dane and amped up his manipulation techniques, and combined with my loneliness, made me walking bait. He must have changed his mind about killing me when he had the car hit me, making sure I got to the hospital in time and luring me back in with fake promises.

All to have an angel/demon hybrid?

What a bastard.

And what an extreme waste of time.

I feel so stupid. But mostly, I'm relieved that I see the truth now. And that he was so desperate, he brought me back here—his greed blinding him and giving me what I needed most.

Nial.

As much as Eden is home and where I want to be, it's Nial who has shown me what it means to love.

I hope I will have an eternity to show him all the ways I intend to love him.

He smiles at me, and I squeeze his hand, hoping he can hear my heart.

"Well, since we're waiting for Gabriel and Jophiel and it's raining...should we have dinner together? Maybe a little music?" I ask.

I'm met with hearty agreement, and we all move to the kitchen, which shrinks considerably with four tall angels with large wingspans, not to mention mine, inside it.

Raphael keeps waving his hand in the air to produce an array of food, and Azrael keeps waving it all away in the next moment, which aggravates Raphael and makes the rest of us laugh. The ease we instantly fall into with one another makes it seem as though no time has passed at all, and throughout the evening, as we prepare food and eat together, talking and laughing and catching up, I know that I'm right where I'm supposed to be.

———

After we've leaned away from the table, too full to eat another bite, we get back on the subject of Dagon. I tell them some of the things that have come back to me, even since sitting here. The car hitting me right after I told him I was done. And then I woke up in the hospital not remembering the fight or how I'd ended up there. Another time, not long before the trip, I was about to leave him again. He'd been abusive, and as I was leaving, I fell down the stairs and woke up with him hovering over me, his face contorted to look like he was devastated.

"How am I remembering this now though? Things I didn't even know in those situations?" I ask.

"Because you're back in Eden and restored. And If he tries to deceive you again, and I have no doubt he will try, you'll see through it," Michael says.

"It's not the only thing you'll see through," Nial says, laughing. "I have a feeling you'll be shocked at the next version of him you see. Has he always presented as a good-looking businessman with flashy clothes and too-white teeth?"

I laugh at Nial's assessment of Dane and think back to the different times in my life I've come across him. He isn't blond every time, but he's handsome and the flashy part has been a common thread. "He does always have really white teeth, now that you mention it."

Everyone laughs.

"And he was a snake when I saw him here before," I say softly. "I don't think I've ever seen him the way you do."

"I've seen the snake," Nial says. "But that's stunning in comparison to how he really looks."

I rub my hands over my arms, feeling chilled, and Nial reaches over and takes my hand.

"Don't be afraid," Azrael says, his voice calm. "The more you know, the stronger you are...you won't fall prey to his tricks any longer."

"I'm glad you all have faith in me...because I haven't done much to earn it," I say.

"You guarded the gate for many years. You and Nial were selected over all of us with the most important job," Raphael says. "Everyone makes mistakes, even celestial beings." He grins and stuffs more food in his mouth.

The wind picks up outside, and I feel a moment of dread when thunder cracks through the sky, a flash of light flooding through the room when lightning follows.

Nial goes to the windows and looks out, his hand moving to his head. He looks at me over his shoulder and then rushes toward me.

"I will do my best to not leave your side, but know that if something happens, you are equipped with everything you need." He moves to the long wooden bench that I've occasionally sat on after a long walk and opens it. I gasp when I see him pull out a sword.

"I used to dream about this sword all the time," I say when he hands it to me. "And you were always there on the edges of my memory, but I could never see your face."

The sword feels like an extension of me. I sigh when I lift it to the light and see the blade flash.

"If you must use this, aim for the heart, and don't let anyone take you to the gate we went out of...I don't think they'd try to take you there anyway. My guess is they're going to attempt to get through the garden gate."

"You're talking like it's more than Dane out there."

"It is. Dagon has brought backup."

The air whooshes out of me, and I try not to let fear get the best of me. The others surround me, assessing the view outside. The sky keeps flashing with lightning, and I squeal with excitement, which seems to startle everyone.

"I just saw Gabriel and Jophiel out there. I'm so excited to see them!" I have the sudden inclination to switch outfits, and instead of taking the time to go to the closet, I imagine the outfit that best serves what I need.

My jewel-encrusted bra is in place, the chain

looping down to my flowy pants...in hot pink because I'm happy.

Nial smiles when he sees me. "There you are," he says.

I reach up to kiss him and hurry toward the glass door, looking back. "Are we ready?"

"Looks like you are," Raphael says, grinning. "Let's go kick some demon ass."

Nial snorts. "Still haven't lost your cheese, have you?"

He shrugs. "The ladies like it."

"Which ladies would those be?" Nial asks, sounding suspicious. His clothes change too, a white tunic and pants similar to mine, and he pulls the sword out of the scabbard at his waist.

"Oh, are you in for a surprise when you get into Eden," he says, lifting his eyebrows.

"Nial has all the surprises he can handle with me," I say, giving them both a dirty look.

Raphael punches Nial in the arm, and Nial grins at me, so proud and full of love, it makes my heart pinch.

"Are we doing this?" I ask.

Now that I've fully woken up, I'm ready for *anything*.

CHAPTER TWENTY-SEVEN

The first thing I notice is the hot breeze. At least thirty degrees hotter than usual, a sauna hits me in the face when I step outside.

Gabriel and Jophiel are in the sky, their swords sinking into the winged demons. Azrael and Raphael take off, surrounding Gabriel and Jophiel and letting them rest while they annihilate the creatures surrounding them.

Michael makes a quiet sound, a bird call, and in front of us, Dagon walks toward us, with four demons on either side of him. I don't know how I know it's Dagon because I've never seen him look like this. But the way he stares at me hungrily, his now beady eyes piercing through me, is my first clue.

I laugh when I see his brown jagged teeth and he frowns.

"Too-white teeth," I say under my breath to Nial, and he snickers. "Guess we know his weak spot."

Dagon advances, his posture arrogant, as if he's still got the beauty of Dane covering him, and when he stands within six feet of me, along with his posse, Michael, Nial, and I draw our swords.

Dagon's head tilts. "What's all this? Are we not capable of having a civilized conversation?" he says.

"If you wanted civilized, you wouldn't have rained demons down on our home and interrupted our peace," I spit out.

His eyes narrow and his tongue stretches out to wet his dry, scaly lips. "You see them," he says simply.

"I see them, and I see *you*." I take a step closer, and he flinches slightly before straightening, some of his bravado returning.

The creatures on either side of him run toward Michael and Nial, and Dagon and I face off. Nial falters next to me, worried, and I shake my head, not looking at him as I say, "Don't worry about me. Fight."

He slashes his sword and gets one right away, but there are three more that are on him.

Dagon grins and takes a few steps toward me. I hold my sword out and place it against his chest. He walks through it and my eyes widen. I wasn't expecting that. The next thing I know, his hands are on my waist, and he lifts us into the sky. I squirm and kick, and his breath smells like a sewer against my ear.

"How did you ever mask that breath?" I yell. "You are so rank. No wonder I wanted to get away from you in every life."

He doesn't like that, his hand yanking my hair back as he sinks his teeth into my neck. I manage to elbow him in the gut, and that knocks him back just enough for me to turn and knee him in the balls. He lets out an *oomph* and drops a few feet, giving me a chance to fly quickly toward Nial. He's just fighting one now. I drop to the ground and look around for Dagon. I feel him before I see him, and my skin crawls as his hands squeeze my body, my pants ripped off of me. I turn, trying to see him to fight him off, when I feel him attempt to enter me. I start stabbing what I can't see, and he makes another strangled sound, this one sounding near the ground.

"You are not touching me again. Do you hear me?" I yell.

I stab where the sound came from, and his

form comes into view again. He's huddled into a ball, trying to protect his precious pitiful privates from being mutilated.

I loom toward him with my sword, and he puts his hand over his face, peering at me through his fingers. "Don't hurt me. You got me." He shows me the cut in his side. "See? I won't hurt you."

I take a step back, and he sighs in relief, but I see the look in his eyes. And his next comment proves I'm right.

"We've had some good times together. It can be good again, you know. We were happy." He tries to look sad, and I just shake my head.

"You know I see how pathetic you are now, right? Not only how hideous you are, but every lie that's come out of your mouth. Every time you hurt me, every time you wiped my memory, every time you kept me from where I was supposed to be and who I was supposed to be with...*I see it all*." I shake with fury, and he shudders, his scrawny little body trembling with fear. "Stand up and fight. We end this today."

"I don't want to fight you," he says.

"That's funny. You sure wanted to hit me when I was under your foul presence and not as strong as you."

"Our child could rule the world, Seraphina. We would never have to bow before anyone ever again. The world would be at *our* feet."

"Stand. Up. And. Fight." My words are controlled, but there is a roar beneath them that makes the ground rumble.

He stands up, shaking. "I'm harmless now. Look at me."

I shake my head. "You are not capable of the truth," I repeat the words Nial said about him and am so glad I listened because in the next moment, Dagon's body shifts and he stands towering over me, his body long and muscular and beautiful. His hair is down to his waist and his legs are like thick tree trunks.

But I don't believe in this version of him, not when he's been exposed and brought to his lowest.

I laugh, and his eyes gleam red. "Nice try," I tell him.

I hold out my sword and let her strength sing through my veins. Flames burst out of the sword, and Dagon shrinks in fear as I sink it into his gut and pull it out as he slowly begins to drop. Right before he hits the ground, I bury it into his heart. Blood seeps out of his mouth and his wounds, and he stares at me in shock, his body reverting to the vile creature. He begins shaking again, but this time his air is leaving him, as flames slowly engulf him.

"If you ever find your way into another life, don't come looking for me," I yell, backing away. "Or do, and I'll just kill you then too." I grin as he gasps his one last breath.

CHAPTER TWENTY-EIGHT

NIAL

I fight with one eye on Phina. Just as I think I've got the last demon, a new one pops up like an aggravating gnat. Phina seems to be holding her own with Dagon, and I know she wants to handle him, but I'm a little paranoid of letting her out of my sight just yet.

And I will never trust that grotesque incubus.

Dagon's greatest skill is flipping the truth and making you believe his lies, and as I stab my sword in the last demon in front of me, I watch as he tries to feign sadness. I stalk toward them as she yells at him to stand up and fight, and the way she faces him like a true warrior is a sight to behold.

I'm in awe as Phina's sword bursts into flame. It's as if the two of them never left, her and her flaming sword, standing watch over the Garden of Eden. A flaming sword took our place when we were banished, flashing back and forth to ward off anyone who tried to get in, but before her plane crashed, the fire of the sword went out. It's how I knew something was wrong.

My eyes blur with tears as I see her sink the final blow into Dagon. And the minute he stops breathing, the skies clear and order is restored.

Phina turns and sees me and starts walking toward me, her face streaked with tears as she laughs and cries, her hand still gripping the sword. She lifts it and puts it in her sheath, the flames dissolving into embers, and falls into my arms.

"How do you feel?" I ask her.

"Like I'm finally home."

"This is where you want to be?" I ask, grinning as I smooth her hair away from her face.

"Where you are is where I want to be."

I kiss her, my heart and my soul putty in her hands, and the sounds of cheering and then a foghorn blasts in our ears.

"Are we sure we're glad Raphael's back though?" I make a face.

"Hey, I heard that," he yells.

Phina's face falls back, and I lean in to kiss her neck, her jawline, her lips. "I love you," she whispers.

"For a thousand lifetimes. Will you stay with me through the next thousand lifetimes though? So I don't have to love you from afar?" I ask against her mouth.

"And beyond." She puts her hands in my hair and smiles up at me. "I cannot wait."

"What do you say we take this celebration into the Garden?"

Phina turns to see Gabriel and Jophiel standing there, and she lets go of me and runs to hug them. And I do the same. Gabriel's spiky white hair and white eyes rimmed in black usually give him an intense look, but he grins like a proud papa, his arms around us both as we walk toward the gate. Jophiel leads the way, her bright yellow hair glowing in the night sky.

Once we reach the gate, the dawn of a new day is beginning. Jophiel stands to the side and motions for Phina to open the gate. She steps forward and puts her hands in front of the gate, and it opens. She looks at me, her eyes bright and hopeful. She takes her sword out of her sheath, and it moves into position. I do the same with mine and it takes the other side. We all step through the gate and close it, and the swords' flames burn bright as they flash back and forth, where no evil will prevail.

We walk through the garden, and it feels so good to be back here, where everything is right with the world again, and I'm with the people I love. And when I look at Phina, the euphoria on her face, the true elation to be where she belongs, is almost more than I can take.

"Your love has stood the test of time," Jophiel says, turning to us and taking us both by the hand. "And the darkness that you drove out today cannot harm you again. You are free of it, and we welcome you here. What Dagon tried to rob from you— your home, your love, your mind—will now be restored to you. Dagon tried to gain the upper hand so he could usurp the Almighty, but he did not win. The Almighty is near, and I know you can feel the blessing." She smiles, and sparkles of light emanate from her.

A sense of peace fills me and Phina leans her head against my arm, humming out a sigh.

"Are you too weary from all the excitement?" Michael asks.

"Are you kidding? I feel like I could run a million miles," Phina says.

We all laugh.

"I suspect you'll be feeling that energy for quite a long time, making up for all the time you weren't flying and defeating a small army of demons," Raphael says. "You lucky, lucky man," he says to me under his breath.

I shove him in the chest, but he jumps back quickly, laughing.

"She only has eyes for you, and we all know it," he adds. "I just need to find someone who looks at me with even *half* that much devotion...and energy..."

I laugh, knowing exactly how lucky I am.

And I plan to enjoy every second of any energy Phina hopes to burn off with me.

CHAPTER
TWENTY-NINE

We leave the big house where Gabriel and Jophiel live, stomachs full and tight from laughing so much, hearts light from such happiness. We spent the whole day there, and now it's almost dark. Once we reach the end of their long path, we take a left and walk until we reach a serene beach with a beautiful white house suspended on stilts over the water.

"This wasn't here before," I say, excitedly. "Have you seen this before now?"

"I was dreaming it up after lunch. We used to

spend time on this beach, and the others were okay if we claimed it. They all thought of it as ours anyway."

"It's spectacular."

"You haven't even seen inside yet." He puts his arms around me and presses my back to his chest as we look up at the house.

"I may be adding a few touches of my own," I tell him, laughing.

"I was hoping you would, although we might have to compromise a bit if you changed the library. I put a lot of thought into what we'd both like in there…"

"Oh no, it was perfect. But I did make the bathtub and shower a lot bigger…and the bed." I giggle. I turn and hover in the air, coming face to face with him. "Can I have the full tour later? And you take me to the library now?" I grin and lean in to kiss him before taking off, my wings tucked to my back as I glide up in one long swoop.

"You comin'?" I tease.

"Right behind you…where I will be happy to spend all of my days," he says.

We run through the halls, while I exclaim over brief glimpses of what we pass, but I stay focused on getting to the library. I reach it first and wait for him before going in. When we enter the room, I turn around and around, my hands to my heart.

"It's a dream," I whisper. "Truly a dream."

"It is a masterpiece if I do say so myself." He smirks.

He has every right to be cocky. It's unbelievable. It's sleek yet cozy with curves in the walls lined with books, ornate woodwork giving that special detail to an already beautiful room. A white velvet chaise lounge sits in front of the windows, large enough for two to read there comfortably.

"I cannot wait to spend time in here with all these books, but what really grabbed my attention was this." I walk over to the swing hanging from the ceiling, the pulley lined with feathers. White leather and a nice pillow at the top and stirrups for me to put my feet in while he—well, the possibilities are endless.

"What made you think to include this?" I ask, circling the contraption.

His eyes are heated already, and I eye him back hungrily, ready for whatever he has in mind for me.

"It seems that we'll have a lot of time on our hands—an eternity is a very long time, you know—and this thing can go at least a hundred different ways."

"Fascinating," I whisper, reaching out and taking his hand. "What should be the first position we try?"

"I thought Air Rider would be a good one for

the two of us. We can also take this to the air some-time and make it official." His voice is husky and he's trying not to laugh, but I feel the heat all the way to my toes.

"I like the sound of that." I unbutton his shirt and let it fall to the ground. His pants are next, and he lies back on the swing, positioning one section behind his back and the other on his upper thighs. I strip out of my clothes, having covered up more on our walk to the gate earlier. I watch the way his body reacts to seeing mine, loving the way I crave him too. As soon as I'm close enough, he lifts me up until I'm straddling him, and he lines us up before thrusting into my wet heat.

With every move, the swing bobs, allowing him to penetrate deeper and deeper.

"What a great idea," I tell him, already breath-less. He has that effect on me.

"I'm certain we can find many, many ways to enjoy this," he says, kissing me deep.

We rock and spin and bob, and I lose my mind a few times right there on the swing. When we realize we still have a whole house to christen, we take a break from the swing and move to the chaise lounge.

I intend to make every moment count with him.

Eternity is not long enough.

*After sending them out, the LORD God stationed
mighty cherubim to the east of the Garden of Eden.
And he placed a flaming sword that flashed back
and forth to guard the way to the tree of life.*
~Genesis 3:24

Thank you so much for reading
Falling in Eden!
This book is part of LEGENDS AND
LOVERS, a collection of dark legends and
star-crossed love stories from nineteen
bestselling authors. Woven with mystery and
magic, love and lore, romance and suspense,
this multi-author collaboration promises to
make your heart pound and keep you reading
late into the night.
Discover all the books in the series
at *legendsandlovers.com!*

Acknowledgments

Adriane Leigh, thank you for coming up with this fun Legends and Lovers idea and for organizing all of it! You're the best. XOXO

Maria from Steamy Designs, thank you for creating this amazing cover. I LOVE IT.

The Love Chain, Laura Pavlov and Catherine Cowles—thank you for all the love! I love doing life with you and trying to figure out all the book things together! Thanks for being a safe place no matter what. I could not love you more.

Christine Estevez, thank you for loving this story, and thank you for your help each and every day! Most of all, thank you for your friendship. Love you!

Nina Grinstead, thank you for your invaluable wisdom and for being so wonderful. I just love you...did from the first time we met and it only grows!

Thank you, Valentine PR! Kim Cermak, Christine Miller, and Sarah Norris, thank you especially for putting up with me and for the awesome work you do! So grateful.

Tosha Khoury, thank you for dropping everything to read my books and for always telling me the truth. My sister bff, love of my life. <3 Grateful for you forever and ever, amen.

Christine Bowden, thank you for being an exceptional human always. I love you so much. Thanks for still reading my books after all this time and for your encouraging love.

Courtney Nuness, thank you for cheering me on, whether it's my gooey cake or a good hair day or a book. Court, the beautiful Court, I love you always.

Claire Contreras, I love our conversations. I feel like there's maybe nothing we haven't covered but that we'll always come up with more. Love you. XO

Kalie Phillips, thank you for reading WHATEVER I write and still hanging in there for more. I'm so grateful for you. Love you!

Anna Gomez, Kell Donaldson, Korrie Kelley, Savita Naik, Terrijo Montgomery, Darla Williams, Priscilla Perez, Layne Deemer, thank you for your encouragement and the love. I love you all. And for those who are part of Asters on a regular basis— you're the best!

Tarryn Fisher, thank you for talking me into hitting publish when you did. Thanks for doing life with me and for all the love. I love you so. #likeananimal

Dad, goodness, I hope you're not reading any more of my books, but if you are, know that I love you so much. I love that you're a hardcore reader like me and that Mama was too.

Troi and Phyllis, love you! Get after those books of yours. XO

Nate, Greyley & Kira, and Indigo, my favorites of all time, I love you so much. Thanks for putting up with all the book ideas, covers, and titles I bring to the table, for pushing me to do what I love, and for being the best family I could ask for. This time with you is priceless. Winston and Elton, that goes for you too. <3

And thank you to every reader, every blogger, every author who took the time to share posts about this book and to review it! I'm so grateful for each one of you.

XO,
    Willow

ABOUT THE AUTHOR

Willow Aster is a USA Today Bestselling author and lover of anything book-related. She lives in St. Paul, MN with her husband, kids, rescue dog, and grandcat.

For ARCs, please join my master list: https://bit.ly/3CMKz5y

For behind-the-scenes of my books and freebies every month, sign up for my newsletter: http://www.willowaster.com/newsletter

www.willowaster.com

Manufactured by Amazon.ca
Bolton, ON

26092407R00116